W. H. H. Murray

Lake Champlain and it's Shores

W. H. H. Murray

Lake Champlain and it's Shores

ISBN/EAN: 9783742819840

Manufactured in Europe, USA, Canada, Australia, Japa

Cover: Foto ©Andreas Hilbeck / pixelio.de

Manufactured and distributed by brebook publishing software
(www.brebook.com)

W. H. H. Murray

Lake Champlain and it's Shores

LAKE CHAMPLAIN

AND

ITS SHORES .

BY

W. H. H. MURRAY

AUTHOR OF " ADVENTURES IN THE WILDERNESS," " DAYLIGHT LAND,"
" ADIRONDACK TALES," " MAMELONS," " UNGAVA," ETC.

———

BOSTON
DE WOLFE, FISKE & CO.
365 WASHINGTON STREET

C. J. PETERS & SON,
TYPOGRAPHERS AND ELECTROTYPERS,
145 HIGH STREET, BOSTON.

DEDICATION.

BECAUSE OF HIS ADMIRATION AND AFFECTION
FOR LAKE CHAMPLAIN AND HIS SERVICES IN BRINGING IT
INTO POPULAR NOTICE; BECAUSE OF HIS HIGH STANDING AND NOBLE-
NESS OF NATURE; AND BECAUSE HE IS MY FRIEND,
I DEDICATE THIS LITTLE VOLUME TO THE

Hon. J. Gregory Smith.

THE AUTHOR.

BURLINGTON, VT.,
1880.

CONTENTS.

INTRODUCTION.

I HAVE prepared this volume in the interest of history and of pleasure both. In the first place I desired to collect and popularize certain facts and incidents which have remained hidden from general observation or published in such a disconnected manner as to be practically useless in the cause of correct knowledge. I wished also to correct certain errors of place and name and conclusion that writers and speakers have invariably fallen into when mentioning matters connected with Lake Champlain and its shores. Above all else I desired to call national attention, especially that of scholars and students in our colleges and public schools, to the historic events which had occurred

in this valley, and their intimate connection
with American liberty and civilization; for
it seemed to me that these would be in-
tensely interested in a theme so significant,
and to which their attention may never have
been directly called. I had at the start a
larger work in contemplation, and for years
have been collecting material for it; but
under the present condition of the public
taste in respect to letters it is not likely
that such a work would be commercially
profitable to a publisher; and as we are
now living, as regards literature, in a *régime* of
dollars and cents, when mental efforts are
weighed in the same scale with sugar and
hams, the question which decides all scholarly ventures is, whether it will pay or not.
The historical section of this little volume
should, therefore, be regarded by the reader
as a suggestion rather than a treatment of
the subject.

I desired, furthermore, to commend this

lake to the favor of the American people, not only because of its historic connections, but because while it stands at present comparatively unoccupied, it nevertheless supplies to them, for the purpose of recreation, one of the most desirable pleasure resorts of the country. Having seen most of the localities of the continent noted for their beauty, I can but declare that I know no other spot which for loveliness of appearance, majesty of scenery, and varied resources of entertainment can compare with Lake Champlain. Nature has signalized and history has emphasized it with such charms and attractions that it challenges the attention and invites the presence of all who love the one or are impressed with the other. As among waterfalls there is but one Niagara in the country, so among lakes there is but one Champlain. Geographically connected as it is with the Horicon and the Hudson on the south and the St. Lawrence on the north;

with the Adirondacks and the White Mountains on the west and east, it invites the visitors of these celebrated localities to the spectacle of its marvellous beauty and the view of its historic places and ruins.

THE AUTHOR.

A PREPARATORY CHAPTER.

OUTDOOR LIFE.

THE tendency of our times is to quit the fields, and crowd into the street; to desert the hillside, and pore over a book in some study. The tide of our civilization sets towards the cities. The drift of the age is all urban. We are a nation of city-builders, and the artificial characteristics of city population are fast printing themselves upon the body of society. We are tattooed from head to foot with city impressions, and if these impressions could only be repeated in color, we should see how few of the markings are natural, and how many are the result of art and the skill of human appliance. The problem of government on the continent is the problem of controlling the population of our cities. The republic to-night. in the number of its votes, is not agricultural and rural, it is commercial, mechanical, urban. The cities of America already dictate the policy of America. Even religion is growing to be metropolitan. The time was when the great lights of theology and of pulpit power were country pastors. The time was in Connecticut, when Porter at Washington, and Bellamy at Bethlehem, and Beecher on Litchfield Hill, directed the religious life of Connecticut churches. To-day the pastors in those villages exercise no appreciable influence on the morals or the religious opinions of the State. To-day, the best preachers, by a tendency of the time that no power can resist, are drawn into the cities. The best thinkers are either in, or grouped around, our universities; and the social life, the intellectual stimulus and the religious characteristics of our universities are moulded into the form of metropolitan customs and associations. The home-life of the nation has been influenced to the same extent and in the same direction. The homesteads of New England have passed, or are fast passing, from the control of New England men and women, into the hands of those of foreign extraction.

It is safe to say that the old New England home-life is already a thing of the past. Even the fireplace, which had in it such elements of cheerfulness and good health that it would seem able to withstand any innovation, has now become such a rarity as to be a matter of pleasurable surprise when you enter a house and see a cheerful fire burning. These things are straws which show the drift of the current and the swiftness of it. In these changes are written the history of a revolution — a revolution in manners, in usage, in habits of living; and such a revolution is more radical, far-reaching, and momentous in its influence than one which is expressed in war and battle. The roar of cannon and the gleam of swords are less significant of change than the destruction of New England homesteads, the bricking-up of New England fireplaces, and the doing away with the New England well-sweep; for these show a change in the nature of the circulation itself, and prove that the action of the popular heart has been interrupted, modified, and become altogether different from what it was.

Now city life means indoor life. Cities are made up of houses, and composed of buildings that men build. And those that live in cities, from the necessities of their condition, live in houses. From the houses where they sleep, men pass to the houses where they work, and they take the shortest cut from the one to the other and bribe the inventiveness of the age to supply them with the quickest locomotion. Our amusements as well as our business are all within-doors. The games which our children play are parlor games; and the games which the children of a country play photograph the future life of the country. The amusements of a nation more than its business shape the character of it. The difference between the recreation of a Parisian and the recreations of a Swiss mountaineer portray the difference between the two men; and as they differ so will their children. Their virtues even are unlike, both in nature and the mode and sphere of their exercise. The one is strong, hearty, healthy; the other is weak, suave, feverish. The one is impulsive, the other constant.

The great lack of our cities — the lack which should challenge our gravest attention — is seen in the absence of playgrounds for our children. What every American city needs are places where the boys can skate and coast, and race and wrestle; where the girls can romp and gather flowers, and hold their sociables under the shadow of trees and on the banks of streams. The absence of these facilities which are essential to the proper development of boyhood and girlhood — for the real health of their bodies, the growth of their minds, and the purity of their morals — will tell fatally on the rising generation. You can't grow trees of tough fibre without the help of wind. No richness of soil, no sunniness of exposure, no nursing of skilled arboriculture will give unto the hickory the fineness of its fibre, or to the oak its stalwart strength. It must bear the pressure of currents; it must stand up against the violence of atmospheric commotion; it must have charged into it the conservatism of frost and the pliancy which comes from movement and moisture. You can't grow strong trees under a glass roof. No more can you grow

boys into strong men by any indoor culture.
Neither the care of love, nor the skill of medicine, nor the appliances which money can buy,
nor any system of schoolroom education will
give unto them those forces and inculcate those
principles which they need when the tasks and
duties of manhood are laid upon them. They
need the freedom of the fields and the stream.
They must breathe of the strength of the wind.
They must receive through the pores of their
skin the ministry of the sun. They must have
the discipline of weariness and risk. They
must be strengthened in their courage by opposition, and learn self-mastery and self-respect
under the provocation of active companionship
with nature and with their mates. I take no
stock in the babying of boys. I resent the
fashion which makes little girls nothing but
animated dolls. The girls that make the best
women, the best wives, the best mothers, are
the girls that are educated in the school of
industry, in the school of service for others; in
that school in which every scholar has his own
burden to bear and is taught how to bear it.

The beauty of natural life is seen in its

liberties. The tyranny which is the worst form
of tyranny is not the tyranny of the strong,
gauntleted hand, but the tyranny of soft
fingers and gloved palms. Luxury is the
heaviest oppression. Boys and girls are ruined
by what they have, by the lavishness of paren-
tal giving, and not by what they lack. The
women that gave most of us birth, and en-
dowed us with their strength, were women that
worked themselves, and whose doing day by
day and week by week made them strong.
The faces back of us that we love most are the
wearied faces, wearied in their services of love,
wearied in nightly vigils and daily ministrations of actual toil.

There is a ministration also which comes to
the soul of one who lives the outdoor life of
nature. The best wisdom of the world has
never been printed. You can't find it in books.
It has never been translated out of the sky, the
flower, the white passing cloud, the running
stream, and the rustling leaf into words.
Knowledge can be obtained out of books. But
knowledge is only the gross, fleshly body of
wisdom ; and the soul of wisdom, the fine spirit

of intelligence, the divinity of fact, and law,
and life expressive of persons, and force, and
things, abhors the crash of the printing-press.

The discoveries that have lifted the world
were not made by book-readers. Galileo questioned the heavens, and from amidst their
starry splendors, from the still distance of their
dim depths, they answered him with the stupendous assertion that the earth moved through
space. The scholars of the world laughed at
him; the ecclesiastics arraigned him, and, with
the threat of torture, made his lips declare a
lie. But he knew then, and we know to-day,
that the heavens had not lied to him, and that
nature had taught him a wisdom worth all the
libraries of the world. Watt did not get the
hint of the marvellous energy of compressed
steam from poring over books. He questioned
a natural force, and that force revealed unto
him a secret mighty enough to revolutionize
civilization.

Newton found the power which propels the
machinery of the universe, hanging on the
bough of an apple-tree — saw in the force of an
apple the mystery of motion, and an answer to

questions which had puzzled the wise from the birth of the race. Franklin opened up a new world of knowledge while playing with a kite. The winds lifted his interrogation into the heavens, and the heavens answered it with the revelation of a hitherto unknown power — a power which to-day makes thought universal, and brings the remotest parts of the earth face to face. Men read the books of Agassiz, but he himself read wisdom in the fin of the fish, the wing of the bird, and the living organisms of nature. Audubon spent forty years in field and forest, on the seashore and the banks of streams to show scholars how profound was their ignorance of what was perched on their house-tops, confined in their cages, and building nests in every thicket and grove in the land.

And so I might go on with the enumeration, but of what avail would it be? I have said enough to give your minds the direction of my thought. You can see how little of that knowledge which is profitable, which is essential to civilization itself has come from the study of the library, and how much has come from the great outdoors. The true library to read — the library on whose shelves and in whose alcoves is not a useless volume — is the library of nature. Her facts are recorded in forces; are apprehended in the operations of laws; are written in the structure of animals, and visible in the nature of things. And if one is ambitious after knowledge; if he craves facts; if he hungers after information, then let him leave his house, turn his back on his books, and go where great men have always gone, — to the very source and fountain-head of accurate intelligence, — and drink of the flowing streams as they flowed.

But there is a finer knowledge than that which relates to the mind. It is the knowledge of that which has for its object the inspiration and building-up of the soul.

Now, the weak point in American society to-day is its artificiality. The life of many is but a vain show. They seem to be what they are not. They surround themselves with splendid appearances, while they themselves are ignoble. They purchase a magnificent frame, within the golden borders of which they insert a daub and call it a work of a master. We have made money too fast in the last forty years. We have developed the material prosperity of the country too rapidly not to have had the standard by which the worth and worthlessness of things are measured inverted. Wealth stands for worth. Beauty of face makes good the absence of beauty of soul. Sensationalism in the pulpit draws better than true oratory. Shystering in law pays as well as a solid legal ability. Spread-eagle and buncombe in Congress, and nimble facility for voting money in behalf of great " internal improvements," and of voting money, too, in behalf of one's self, carry the suffrage of a district against patriotism, ability, and unimpeachable character. There is a craving desire on the part of everybody to seem to know more than they know, to be worth more than they are worth, to look beautiful when nature has made them plain, to talk knowingly about books that they have never read ; and this spirit of artificial living, this tendency to exaggerate one's self, has passed its virus into the very blood of American life.

We know that every age and every nation

has its characteristic vice, as every face has its prominent feature. The vices of nations are personal and distinctive. History will emphasize this suggestion to your memory. The vice of Rome was military glory, an inordinate thirst for empire, a craving for universal power. She tossed her eagles into the air and charged them to draw the line of their flight to the boundaries of the world. They did. But wherever they flew, they flew with dripping talons, and the shadow of their wings as they passed over peoples and kingdoms was to those who dwelt underneath the shadow of death. That was her vice, and it finally slew her with its own sword.

The vice of Greece, the land of sun and song, was worship of the human body. Greece deified the physique, idolized the human structure, and bowed in adoration before the god her wit and care and culture had made. For its brow she wreathed her laurels, in its praise she sang her songs, and to perpetuate its beauty and glory she wrought, with a thousand educated chisels, her matchless marbles. Her deities were only large men and large women with majestic faces and perfect limbs and beautiful forms. Her vice was poetic, was refined, was spirituelle, but none the less vice. Her gods were mortal, and of course the worshipers could not outlive the gods. She pushed the triumph of her civilization to the limit of the possible as regards human development. It rose like a rocket to the apex of its flight, burst in the day of Pericles in a shower of glory, then faded forever from the sky.

The vice of Spain was bigotry. She made a pride of her narrowness. The Spaniard would not investigate, and in the arrogance of his ignorance he forbade investigation. Into his narrow mind the dream of a new world could not enter. His priest-ridden intellect could not admit to itself the mighty movement of the heavens, nor his senses acknowledge that the earth beneath his feet was forever rolling on in its sublime career. He scoffed at Columbus, and threatened Galileo with the rack. He advertised himself as the bigot of the ages.

The vice of France, since the time of Charlemagne, has been fickleness. France has been like a sea, blown upon and tossed. France has

been like a ship running in a gale, crowded
with canvas, without an anchor on deck, and
without a helm. Her career has been rapid,
but eccentric — now empire, now kingdom, now
republic, now anarchy. To-day blindly obe-
dient to priests; to-morrow, a total disregarder
of all religious convictions. France has been
as a man subject to intermittent insanity. To-
day she is sane; to-morrow she is kept at her
work at the point of the bayonet.

The vice of Germany is scepticism — the
scepticism which is born of libraries, which is
breathed by those who spend their days and
their nights in the dim recesses of misty
alcoves; the scepticism which comes from the
over-reading of books, and too little and too
narrow observation of men; the scepticism
which the specialist is exposed to, whose mind
is forever condensed into one ray and focalized
upon one minute point; who knows one truth,
but knows not the relations which it sustains to
a thousand other truths, and who has never
mastered the sublime harmony of the arranged
whole.

The vice of England — well, what is it? It

is selfishness. The selfishness of fifty thousand landholders who will not part with an acre that the millions living around them may own a square foot of the soil which the sweat of their industry moistens and irrigates to fruitfulness; the selfishness of hereditary aristocracy jealous of its honors — honors which they have never fought for, but which have been transmitted to them; of fame which they have never won on the sea nor the battle-field; of immense wealth, to whose full coffers their hands have never contributed a dollar. A selfishness which regards the whole world as only a huge sponge, providentially made and filled with the moistening of riches for the British fingers to grasp and press the golden contents into British coffers.

And so I might question all nations, from the beginning of history down to the present time, and we should see that each nation and each age has had its characteristic, prevailing, and distinguishing vice. Well, what is the vice of America? It is not military glory as was Rome's; for we do not thirst for conquest, and our young men prefer the employment of peace to the risk and the deprivations of war. It is not deification of the physique. I wish we regarded our bodies with greater reverence, and gave unto them the attention of finer care. It is not bigotry; for we are liberal and tolerant. Twenty denominations and twice as many creeds live at peace within our borders. It is not fickleness; for we are stable. Through the most radical and rattle-brained Yankee in New England there runs a broad, strong streak of conservatism. Blood will tell; and the old Puritan blood, the constitution-loving blood of old England, the blood which wrung the great Magna Charta from King John, and gave to the world constitutional liberty — this blood, which flows in our veins to-day, gives unto us all a sense of caution; a jury-like patience in hearing both sides of a case; a determination not to jump before we look. I never saw a Yankee yet that had not at least ten-twentieths of old fogy blood in his veins. I never yet saw a Yankee as impulsive as an Irishman, or as wild-headed as a Frenchman, or as subject to spasms and fits as an Italian. It is not scepticism; for we are reverent and believing,

I think I may say credulous. The Yankee loves his creed as the Irishman loves a cudgel. It enables him to whack a man religiously. The old Adam in him, which his piety forbids him to express in profanity, he can let out in theological argument. The amount of irreligiousness which a Maine Baptist and a New Hampshire Congregationalist can work out of themselves in the course of a forty-minute religious discussion of their respective tenets can never be computed by the resources of the calculus.

What, then, is the characteristic vice of America? What is the distinctive weakness of our character? What is the prevailing shame of the day? It is *artifice*. The American character is not a genuine one. It is a made-up character — a character based upon seeming, not being. This vice is spread through all the thousand and one possible expressions of society. You can see it crop out everywhere. Men love to seem to be rich, richer than they are; and to keep up appearances they sacrifice integrity, peace of mind, domestic happiness, and even commercial honor itself. Women join in this feeling of rivalry. They dress for appearances and not for comfort and health. Their standard is to outshine some one, to outdo some one, and to cast into the shade some more modest or more truthful neighbor. Girls love to be thought handsomer than they are, and leave the true road which leads the human figure and face up to beauty, health, and that way of life and dress which leads to health. They resort to artificial methods, to art, and contrivance, and wit, whose nature is hypocrisy, and whose ultimate issue can be nothing but mortification and a broken-down constitution. A really frank, open, genuine person is so rarely met with to-day that it is almost dangerous to be so, for such a one is a marked person, and sensible and sensitive people shrink from being remarked upon and gossiped about; and so, from self-defence, as it were, because of the evil usage of the times, even they who would be natural are compelled to adopt the wretched habit of evasion and semi-hypocrisy. This, of course, leads to injurious reticence, and this habit of reticence affects not only social circles injuriously, but every circle. The man of business does not dare to reveal the state of his business, does not dare to say how little capital he is doing business on, and so evasion and deceit, falsehood and pretentiousness, even lying itself, are the inevitable resorts of his policy. These are the things that honeycomb the foundation of credit and charge the air full of suspicion, which trade, having breathed, becomes paralyzed through all her members. Into the same dreadful habit falls the politician who thinks one thing and says another. He knows what is the truth, but he won't say it. He is not frank and open and fair in his talk to his constituents. And so strongly has this habit become settled as a rule and policy among American politicians, that he is called the best politician who can conceal most and deceive most. He who has that which enables him to be a first-class, gilt-edged rascal is called a first-class, successful politician.

And the same tendency can be seen in the pulpit. Many men in the pulpits of the country to-day are not saying their latest thought to their people. If you ask them why, they will tell you because they dare not do it. The man will say, "If I should tell my people what I think about the inspiration of some books of the Old Testament; if I should give them my ideas of the book of Job, such as all scholars know; if I should even enumerate the errors of translation which my acquaintance with Greek and Hebrew have brought me, my church would rise up and demand my dismission, my deacons would charge me with dangerous tendencies, and my brothers in the ministry around about me would among themselves speak of my honesty as folly, and in council declare me an unsafe guide."

The reason why so many preachers are dull is because they are repetitious. There is no fragrance in the flowers they gather week by week for their people, because they are the faded flowers, the withered bouquets that have hung in the theological garrets for a hundred and fifty years. No wonder that the people sniff them and find no pleasure therein; no wonder that they endure preaching rather than love it. There is nothing more strongly demanded by the necessities of the times than

that each preacher should begin to be honest
in dealing with his people, should begin to
appear intellectually conscientious and give
forth to his congregation his latest convictions
of truth, and the result of his latest investigation as a student of truth. The human mind
is a growth, not a substance, and in order that
it may become a power its growth must be kept
before the people. It is like that Apocalyptic
tree of which John dreamed, " which yielded
its fruit every month, and whose leaves were
for the healing of the nations." So a preacher's mind should ripen its monthly fruitage for
the people's taste, and the suggestions which
the winds of occasion would blow down from
its branches, as leaves are blown from the trees,
would be such suggestions as never before came
forth from the branches of the human mind.
And the people who sit under the shadow of
such a ministry find their food ever fresh and
its offerings ever new. And this habit of
speaking out one's latest thought in the ministry would make a minister thoughtful, would
stir a thousand beneficent agitations, and keep
the parish surroundings lively with mental in-

terchanges and spiritual impartments. The man whose parish to-night is calm, but calm with the dead level of mental stagnation, should at once start a breeze in that parish, and stir his people with rippling discussions; and if enemies, if bigotry, if envy seize upon his frankness and his intellectual candor and his spiritual honesty, and strive to convert them into weapons to fight him with, he should stand forth in the might of genuine nature, panoplied in the power of truthful studentship, clothed in the armor of one who speaks what the Lord gives him to say, whether man will hear or forbear. And so acting he would find that danger would cease to be danger, risk would lose its characteristic of peril, and to his own life would come a magnificent growth, and into it his people would grow with him.

I hold that beyond all other men clergymen should live as much as possible out of doors. Like plants they need air, they need sunshine, they need the ministrations of the natural. In this way they become simple, devout, bold, and true. Nature inspires no cowards. Nature begets no pedantry. Nature suggests no bigotry.

The spirit of devotion tabernacles among the hills. Neither saint nor sinner can truly worship God while he sleeps under a shingled roof. Visions of duty, vast, sublime, overwhelming, never come to one who sleeps in a chamber whose measurement is ten by twelve. You must leave your houses, friends, and go forth into the open air. Leave the city and go into the wilderness, and there, far from human habitations, make your bed beneath the stars, and lift your eyes toward the magnificent dome in which they shine, and feel the weight of the immense distances settling on you, or ever you can know the majesty of God or the solemn joy of which the soul is capable when it is lifted heavenward in worship.

Not only is the religious nature developed by outdoor influence, not only does nature develop the spiritual faculties, but the social nature is influenced to an equal extent by her benign power. Nature is full of voices, and they are all happy. Nature never scolds, never chafes, never frets, never worries one. She is full of music, and fun and merriment are her delight. I have lain for many an hour hidden amid her

leaves and her grasses, and seen denizens of
lake and forest act out their natures unconscious of my observation. I have laughed till
tears stood in my eyes to see the playfulness of
her fish and her birds, the gambols and mis-
chievous pranks of her animals.

Now, all men are made to laugh. Every man
can be tickled if you find the right nerve. No
man is so crusty that he won't mellow up at a
picnic, or on a fishing trip, or at a fox hunt.
And the laughing which nature prompts is
never bitter, never cynical. Nature brings out
the real human that lies latent in one, uncaps
the choked-up springs of merriment in the
bosom, and sets the rivulet of laughter flowing.
The laughter of indoor life is smothered, con-
strained, puckered into forms of politeness;
but the laughter of the outdoor life is large
and hearty and thoroughly jolly. "No one
laughs well who doesn't laugh loud," says the
old proverb; and the proverbs of a people are
the wisdom of a people condensed. The fact is,
the funniest laughter is the laughter that one
has alone. It is very well to laugh in company,
for custom and benevolence alike demand it;

but, for the most part, company laughter is
forced. It is a made-up, artificial thing, or else
too slight and decorous to be hearty and adequate. But when the spirit of fun gets into
one when all alone by himself to such an extent
as to fairly possess him, and he sits down and
puts his hands against his sides, and opens his
mouth, and begins to sway backward and
forward until his eyes rain with mirth, and
he fairly wrestles inwardly with his hilarity;
then his laughter is the genuine thing. We live
within-doors too much to be happy. Life
becomes too much of a routine, an exhibition
of one and the same experience. We should
seek more variety. We should open ourselves
up to the exhilaration of incident. We should
go forth and stand in the midst of many
objects, and rejoice our eyes with varied sights
and court contact with the accidental and the
romantic.

In this way we should find refreshment; our
days would tingle with novel sensations, and we
should go to our homes at night as bees fly to
their hives, having visited a dozen fields, and
drawn the sweetness from a thousand flower-

cups. In this way we should become thoroughly healthy; and health is something of which we have all heard, but which few have ever had. They say there is such a thing! Doctors tell us of it, and we pay them for the news, — that is all. Life means eating and sleeping. He who can't eat his food with a relish, — and a goodly amount of it, too, — he who can't sleep soundly at night and late in the morning, does not know what living means. Dyspepsia is a bad bedfellow. The Florentines, after Dante had written his wonderful poem called "The Inferno," used to point him out as he passed along the streets of the city, saying, "There goes the man who has been to hell." A dyspeptic does not need to be a poet to have that remark made of him.

But how glorious is man's estate after he has eaten a good dinner! What solid dignity he has attained! What a satisfactory sense of substantialness is his! How the blessed feeling of fulness adds to his self-respect! And with what an unctuous complacency he can regard his fellow-men! A full stomach is the very mother of sweetest charity. Our fathers had the

insane idea that early rising was proper; but
our fathers — worthy men as they were — had
their delusions, and were victims of misconcep-
tions. They lacked experience, and most of
us know that they were mistaken. I agree with
the witty Frenchman who said that "The only
reason why a man should wake up, was found
in the fact that it enabled him to roll over and
go to sleep again!"

The trouble of it is, friends, people do not
know how to appropriate the influences of
nature. Most people know enough to eat
bread when it is on the table in front of them.
But how to eat the food that is in the wind and
sunshine, that lurks in the fragrance of the
fields, and descends in manna from the sky,
they are ignorant. They are so artificial that
they do not know how to live a natural life.
They go at nature awkwardly. The life at sea-
side hotels and at mountain resorts is too often
a broad farce. No wonder that the humorist and
the satirist find it serviceable for their purpose.
Loafing is not an art; it is a gift; and one of
the best gifts ever bestowed upon man. Indo-
lence in the economy of nature is analogous to

sleep.   A man don't need to be lazy all the
while, but off and on as it were; and by spells;
and the spells shouldn't be too far apart.   I've
seen men in the woods that were as much out
of place as a buzz-wheel in church.   They took
their activity there; they took their energy
there; they took their anxieties there.   They
were always running from spot to spot; always
in full swoop.   They never found a perch nor
settled down.   Now, the human system is like
an engine; it can run fast, run far, run long.
It can do royal service and perform manifold
ministries.   But there comes a time when it
must be slowed up and run into the shop for
repairs.

Now, among all the experiences of outdoor
life — happy and grateful as they are — not one
is more satisfactory than that of sleeping when
your bed is made under the pines, or on the
shore of still lakes, or the banks of murmuring
streams.   Night invites you to repose, and
slumber with gentle movement takes you to
her embrace, as a mother lifts her drowsy child
to the cradle of her bosom.

What a luxury such sleep is, and how little

of the real quality we have in the cities!
Imagine your bed-chamber of odorous bark, and
your bed of pungent boughs. Your couch
made under murmuring trees and within a few
yards of the lazily moving water, whose motions
caress rather than chafe the shore. Stretched
your full length on such a couch, spread in such
a place, the process of falling asleep becomes an
experience. You lie and watch yourself to observe the gradual departure of your senses.
Little by little you feel yourself passing away.
Slowly and easily as an ebbing tide you begin
to pass into the dim and insensible realm beyond
the line of feeling. At last a moment comes in
which you know you are passing over the very
verge of consciousness. You are aware that
you are about to fall asleep. Your cheek but
partially interprets the cool pressure of the
night wind; your ears drowsily surrender the
lingering murmur of beach and pine; your
eyes droop their lids little by little; your nose
slightly senses the odor of the piny air, as you
mechanically draw it in; the chest falls as it
passes as mechanically out, and then — you are
asleep.

The hours pass, and still you sleep on. The body, in obedience to some occult law of force within the insensible frame, still keeps up its respirations; but you are somewhere — sleeping. At last the pine above you, in the deep hush which precedes the.coming of dawn, stills its monotone, and silence weaves its airy web amid the motionless stem. The water falls asleep. The loon's head is under its spotted wing, and the owl becomes mute. The deer has left the shore, and lies curved in its mossy bed. The rats no longer draw their tiny wake across the creek, and the frogs have ceased their croaking. All is quiet. In the profound quiet, and unconscious of it all, the sleeper sleeps. What sleep such sleeping is! and what a ministry is being ministered unto mind and body through the cool, pure air, pungent with gummy odors and strong with the smell of the sod and the root-laced mould of the underlying earth!

We wear out too fast, friends, in this country. We value ourselves too much as if we were bits of machinery. Our lives ascend like the rocket — suddenly explode and leave darkness. They should rise like the sun in gradual ascension,

and decline with the even movement of unex-
hausted powers passing on into other realms.
The problem of the next thirty years, in this
country, is not one of money-making, or of
mind-making, or of soul-making, but the
problem is one that underlies all these, and
on the proper solution of which they all
depend — it is body-making. The births of
the future must be healthy births. What
is the use of bringing cripples into the
world, whether they are crippled in limb, in
stomach, in size and formation of the chest, or
in the blood-system? As a country, we are giving birth to a monstrous number of idiots and
weaklings, and of incipient, embryo criminals.
We can't afford to keep on taxing our indus-
tries with their support, imperilling society with
their violence, or burdening our sympathies with
their presence. Healthy parentage is a solution
of this problem. You can't expect that nervous
motherhood and fevered fatherhood will ever
stand parents to healthy offspring. The laws of
life, about which the average man and woman
are so ignorant, should be taught and obeyed as
the ten commandments, for the next fifty years.

From the great outdoors of God — pure air, strong wind, warm sunshine, plain diet, restful periods of time, and the religious sensitiveness which is closely connected with these influences of Nature, — from these must come our salvation. If we would brick up the flues of our furnaces and put the old-fashioned fire-place, or even the open grate, into the rooms of our houses, we would prove by that act that our civilization, at least, isn't stupid, and that we are too sensible to pay men for killing us with their infernal inventions.

The prime object of architecture should be to bring as much of the outdoors as is possible within-doors. Many American houses are more like ornamental prisons than places of happy residence. We furnish our parlors with everything but fresh air and sunshine. We should have more glass in our windows and screen them less with heavy draperies. You can't import an Axminster so fine, or a damask from Lyons so rich, or a Persian rug so gorgeous, that a streak of warm sunshine on the floor is not, for the purposes of health and happiness, worth them all. No colored marble, or massive

carving of oak and walnut, can make good to
the family life the fireplace of our fathers.
How pure and sweet is the air of a room thus
ventilated! How merry the play of sparks and
the crackling of brands; how cheerful the
glowing coals; how pure the whitened ash;
how genial the issuing warmth. Our sleeping
apartments are often more like cells than chambers. The moment you get below a certain
level of wealth in our cities, the chambers in
which men and women sleep are filled with an
atmosphere dense, damp, and vitiated by being
repeatedly breathed. Those of us who have
lived in camp, who have slept for weeks under
the sky, with the delicious night winds blowing
the odor of lily and pine into our nostrils, can
recall what a smothering sensation we experienced the first night we were compelled to sleep
in the chamber of a house. What a pity that
men will stint themselves of the free air and
lock themselves in from the bright sunshine,
when God has filled the world lavishly with
both. And, above all, what a pity that men
will allow their characters to be shaped by
influences which contract and warp them, when

round about on all sides influences have been
provided calculated to make them wide, generous, and symmetrical.

The brightest sign of the times is the fact
that men and women are beginning to turn
their faces toward the country, and in the good
old-fashioned way, too.   They are beginning to
long for easier lives, for quietness and the
absence of parade.   The gilded bells on the
king's fool are not called music in the palace
to-day, and the gaudy tinsel of his habit is no
longer admired.   It is a hopeful sign when the
wealthy merchant goes back to his ancestral
home, to the little farm where he was born, and
finds enjoyment in once more holding the plough
and mowing the meadow; finds delight in his
sleek oxen, his fine-bred colt, and his herd of
Jerseys.   It is a healthful sign when the woman
of fashion leaves her Saratogas at home, and,
tucking a few necessary articles of comfortable
clothing into her valise, starts with her husband
for a two months' trip in the Adirondacks, or a
month's camping and yachting on Lake Champlain.   It's a healthful sign when our young
men take to boating and ball-playing, when

the pliant rod becomes a fascination, and the long-range rifle a delight. It is a hopeful sign when our young ladies are seen studying flori-culture, learning to sit a saddle properly, acquiring suppleness of limb on graceful skates, and laughingly facing after dinner a four miles' tramp. It is a hopeful sign when men are beginning to ask themselves why the old fire-place was banished and to demand its restora-tion; to ask why the windows of their dwelling are drawn by the architect so small, and why parlors are made so gloomy, more fit for the residence of a hermit than a happy-hearted man. These are the bright evidences, the rosy tints flushing with delicate warmth the sky, which declare that the dawn of a new day is at hand; a day in which we shall get back to the simplicity of nature, shall put a proper value upon the charm of quietness, shall bring the light and purity of the outdoor world into our houses, ay, and into our souls too.

The future will be wiser and better than we have been. It will be more frank, more gen-uine, more manly and womanly. The men and women of the future will be so strong in these

virtues that they will have no motive to be
hypocrites.   Society will gauge people by what
they are intrinsically, and not by what their
fathers gave them, or they themselves have
acquired, of material gain and artificial honor.
By and by we shall stop building houses, and go
to building homes.   Houses can be made of
mortar and brick, of marble and polished
woods, but home can be made only from sunshine, from pure air, from flowers in the windows, from good health and contented minds.
The architects of the next century will take up
the plans of our dwellings, will examine our
tenement houses and say, "How could men and
women have lived in such places?   How could
they have slept in such chambers?   Where could
the sunshine and pure air they needed have
come from?   How could their women have
climbed so many stairs?   How could their
lungs have stood the dust of their furnaces?
Where were the playgrounds for the children?"
They will read of our social habits, peruse the
stories of our hypocrisies, of our frauds and our
shams, and exclaim, "How could they have been
so insincere, so pretentious, so artificial in their

standards of judgment and their action?" They will examine the methods of our cooking, and exclaim, "How could men and women eat such stuff?" Our social habits will be inspected, and it will be the marvel of the future that women should wear such dresses, and men drink such liquors as we do. For the time is coming when common-sense shall be fashion, the frankness of truth be custom, and the simplicity of nature the rule.

Hail to that future! when all that is beautiful, frank, and true in the outdoor realm; all that is mirthful, genuine, and grand in what God has made, shall be introduced into the homes of the world, and imitated in the lives of those who shall then live, and who shall be happy in their living.

LAKE CHAMPLAIN.

PART I.

THE TRADITIONAL AND HISTORIC PERIOD.

CHAMPLAIN, the man, was the last of a long line of navigators, explorers, and heroes, who, with a courage that was of the highest and a perseverance that never faltered for two hundred years, sought for one thing — the Northwest passage. Champlain, the lake, marks the westernmost point of their progress in their heroic seeking. With Champlain the long line ended. And here, in his discovery of the lake, the long seeking of the ancient mariners to find, by sailing westward, the passage to Cathay, ended also. Looking backward from Champlain, what a vista! looking onward from Champlain, what a history! Since Champlain, there have been wars, revolutions, the birth of a mighty government and a developing civilization to which the history of this lake furnishes a key. Before Champlain there were myths, traditions, legends, and suggestive murmurings of knowledge disbelieved for a thousand years.

EARLY TRADITIONS OF AMERICA.

For the mouth of antiquity was not silent in respect to this western world of ours. Hesiod, with his finger on the sounding chord, sang of the gardens of the Hesperides and poured his prophetic song out into the otherwise stirless gloom that hung darkly above the western sea. Plato in faultless prose told the story of Atlantis, that mystical island far beyond the Pillars of Hercules, as his ancestor Solon had received it from the lips of the old Egyptian priests of Sais, who held for truth, beyond doubt, what modern savants, because of their ignorance perhaps, have looked upon as a myth and a mythical catastrophe. The Phœnician sailors swore that their eyes had seen a fair and lovely country lying low down in the western waves, and Carthaginian mariners indorsed

the story and declared that their prows
had touched the golden sands of unknown
islands in unknown seas, whose airs were soft
and sweet with breath of spice and balm.   And
Pytheas, a sailor of Old Greece in the time of
Alexander the Great, told to the wondering
Mediterranean gossips of a country lying to the
north and west, beyond the confines of the
world, whose shores were solid ice and whose
men were clothed like animals.   And Madoc
of Wales — so say the bards — brought back
from voyages strange stories of strange lands
beyond the sunset, and, sailing forth again with
many ships and men, came not back, neither
he, his ships, nor his men, but were swallowed up
by monsters or sunk beneath the fateful waves,
being punished because he sailed beyond the
seas of God.   The airs of the old world fairly
pulse and throb with stirring myth and dark,
weird tales and clear-sounding prophecy of
blessed isles and fragrant lands where dwelt the
gods beyond the sunset and the sunset sea.

Then come the Norsemen — those brave sea-
bees who swarmed out of the stormy north
seeking the honey of plunder.   They swept

down upon England, Belgium, and Normandy, and, buzzing far and near, pushed their fearless flight as far as Sicily and Southern Italy. Then they turned northward and in 874 drew the line of their flight as far as Iceland, six hundred miles from their Norwegian hive, in the wild northern seas. In 1874, the descendants of these old Sea Kings of the North celebrated not the *centennial* but the *millennial* anniversary of their settlement in Iceland.

From Iceland to Greenland is scant two hundred miles. These old Norse sailors were brave and cared no more for wave and tempest than the stormy petrel. We know that King Olaf's ship, the *Long Serpent*, was a hundred and forty feet from stem to stern, and that many of their vessels carried full two hundred men. With such ships such men could go anywhere and laugh — as they did, as they rolled over them and through it — at billows and storm. And in 985 Erik the Red, with twenty-five ships, set sail for Greenland. He doubled Cape Farewell and planted a colony on the eastern coast and called it Eriksfiord. For four hundred years Greenland was a see of papal Rome, and the names of seventeen successive bishops can be read on the records of Holy Church. The colony throve, and where to-day is barren land and inhospitable ice, three hundred farms and villages once flourished.

In the Sagas it is written that in 996 Biarne Herjulfson, a son of Herjulf, a Norse navigator, sailing from Iceland to Greenland, was blown by storm far west, and sighted, amid the fogs that swathed it, a *Newfoundland*. He did not land, but hurried back and told the news to those at home. The story stirred the very souls of those Norse seamen, and four years later, in the year 1000, Leif Erikson, with a stout ship well manned, sailed forth to test the story that Herjulfson had told. They reached an island — Newfoundland, doubtless — and called it Helluland, and then a wooded coast — Nova Scotia — and named it Markland. Then they sailed southward for two days with fair wind, and sighted land and went ashore. It was a pleasant land, and where they landed the wild grapes hung thick from vines that made the trees their arbor railing, and in their joy they called the country Vinland. On this shore they wintered and thus the coast of Massachusetts first knew the white man. All this four hundred years before Columbus.

Then followed Thorwald, brother of Leif Erikson, in 1002. For three years he dwelt in Vinland until war arose between him and the natives, and in battle he was killed. And so the long contest that is not wholly ended yet, although a thousand years have nearly passed, between the white man and the red for the possession of the continent began, and the old Norseman sailor and sea-king was, perhaps, the first white man that fell — the first fruit of that harvest of death that the red sickles of war for all these eight hundred and eighty-eight years have been busily reaping.

Then came others, both men and women, to the same shore, and with them they brought cattle and sheep, and made a brave effort to plant themselves in the country. But the natives fought them, and pirate hordes invaded Greenland itself; and later, a plague, called the Black Death, swept over Europe and Scandinavia like a wave of desolation, and the colony or colonies in Massachusetts perished and eventually passed from the minds of men.

THE OLD-TIME MARINERS.

Then came John Cabot and his son Sebastian. The Cabots were of Venice, — City of the sea, — whose streets are rivers and whose carriages are boats. There was John Cabot born and reared amid gondolas and gondoliers — ships whose sails were colored silk and whose commanders were proud as Doges. The dream of sea-going Venice was ever of the West and of undiscovered lands beyond the setting sun, of which old sailors for a thousand years had told strange stories. In 1496 the Cabots made home in Bristol, England — whether banished out of Venice or having journeyed forth of their own free will, I know not. But being in Bristol, King Henry VII., anxious to win his share of undiscovered lands' and gains, gave him permission to traffic in foreign parts, on condition that the Crown should have one-fifth of all the profits; and so the old Venetian, in 1497, sailed out of the Bristol Channel, hoping to find a western passage to the kingdom of Cathay or China. Having sailed west by north seven hundred leagues, as he computed, he came upon the coast of Labrador, which he supposed to be the eastern shore of China. He landed and planted the Royal Standard and named the country *Prima Vista*. Then did the flag of England first wave above the continent, and the brave man who flung its red folds to the breeze was born in ancient Venice and learned the art of sailing ships upon the tideless sea. From Labrador he sailed southward along the coast six hundred miles, and then returned to Bristol. The king gave him a pension, and empowered him to "impress six English ships, and sailors enough to man them, and go forth again and make farther search for the Northwest passage." But for some cause the expedition never sailed; and of John Cabot we know no more. "He gave England" —as a writer has said — "a continent, and no one of all the English race knows his burial-place." All this a full year before Columbus saw the mainland of America.

The next year, 1498, his son Sebastian, with two ships, sailed from England for China and Japan, still seeking the Northwest passage. He sailed far up what we know as Davis's

Straits, in the month of July, 1498, and was, probably, the first white man that ever saw the marvel of twenty-four hours of continuous daylight. We can imagine the wonder that filled the souls of these old mariners as they sailed onward day after day, without an evening and without a night. Then came the icebergs, floating down like mountain ranges upon him, and he wore ship and sailed steadily southward, still searching along the coast for the Northwest passage, until he came to Chesapeake Bay. Nineteen years later, in 1517, Sebastian entered the bay to which a century later Henry Hudson gave his name, and thence, in subsequent voyages, explored the coast of South America as far as La Plata!

The great fact to remember in this connection is that it was in virtue of these discoveries of the two Cabots—father and son—that England laid claim to all or nearly all of the North American continent. Strange that in all their searching they never found the mouth of the St. Lawrence. We now come to that.

During all these years France had not bestirred herself to find new worlds or claim a

share of those already found.   But at last
Francis I. aroused himself and said, "Shall
Spain, Portugal, and England divide all
America between them and give me no share?
I would like to see the clause in Father Adam's
will which bequeaths that vast inheritance to
them."

There was, at that time, in France a Floren-
tine, skilled in navigation, named Verazzano,
and him Francis sent forth to make discoveries.
He landed first at Chesapeake Bay, and then
sailing northward along the same course which
the Cabots had previously sailed, named the
whole country, whose coast he had skirted only,
New France, and claimed it for Francis.   At
this point we see the conflicting claims of
France and England spring up side by side, and
the cause of the long and bloody wars between
them for the possession of the continent is seen.
In 1523 the strife really began — a strife that
never ceased until Wolfe brought it to a close
two hundred and thirty-two years after on the
Plains of Abraham.

When we remember the size of the vessels in
which these vast voyages and astonishing dis-

coveries were made, the mind is filled with astonishment. Jacques Cartier's ships ranged from sixty down to fifteen tons measurements. Martin Frobisher, that stout old English mariner, pushed northward to the bay that bears his name, in a ship — if such a large-sounding word may be used to describe so small a boat — of only *five and twenty tons!* In 1553, Sir Hugh Willoughby, in a bark of scarce a hundred tons, seeking the path to China, sailed into a Lapland harbor, and there cast anchor forever. For the next year he and all his crew were found in their floating sepulchre, frozen still and solid as marble. Sir Humphrey Gilbert, half-brother to Raleigh, and of the same heroic spirit, sailing homeward from the Newfoundland coast, was overtaken by a great tempest. His ship was called the Squirrel, of *ten tons* burden, and, sitting in the stern-sheets as night came down upon the seething sea, with his Bible on his knees, he called aloud to the crew of his consort sailing by his side, and said, " Fear not, comrades, Heaven is as near by sea as by land." And, saying this, he disappeared from sight.

Henry Hudson, in 1609, in a little craft of thirty tons, called the Half Moon, seeking, like all others, a way to China, penetrated the depths of Hudson's Bay, and wintered amid its awful cold. In the spring, he, with his son and seven other faithful souls, were turned adrift by his mutinous crew, and never again were they heard nor seen by men. The mighty sheet of water that bears his name is both his grave and monument.

In 1603 Samuel Champlain, in two little barks, of *twelve* and *fifteen* tons burden, pushed boldly out from the French coast, crossed the Atlantic safely, and returned to prepare another voyage!

During all this period of knowledge and ignorance both — knowledge on the part of those who had sailed and seen; ignorance on the part of those who had stayed steadfastly at home, made books and read them, and knew nothing save what their narrow, local, and egotistic knowledge of their own country and literature gave them: a period covering a thousand years at least — the fated lake now known as Lake Champlain lay stretched between its amphitheatre of hills like some ancient arena, awaiting, through the still dark hours of night, the coming of dawn, the struggle, and the audience. We say fated : for on no other single body of water on the globe, so far as known to history or tradition, have so many battles been fought, so many brave men died, such mighty issues been settled by the sword, or such momentous questions— as judged by their connection with the government and development of the human race — been decided by the arbitrament of arms. For here on this lake the two great and antagonistic interpretations of Christianity met, in the armed representatives of two warlike races, face to face, and, for a hundred years, the fierce struggle lasted without intermission, save when, at intervals, like two strong wrestlers, equally matched, by mutual consent they released their grip each on the other, and stood apart for a space to renew their breath and summon up their powers for a longer and deadlier clinch. For it must be remembered that it was not in Germany or Geneva, at the Hague or among the mountains of Southern France, that Protestantism gained its everlasting

triumph over its Papal rival, but here between
the Green Mountains and the Adirondack peaks
and on the shores and waters of Lake Champlain was the final and decisive contest between
these two mighty and inherently hostile forces
waged — a contest which gave to Protestant
thought and its resultant liberty the civic possession of a continent, and, through its developing civilization, inspired by its own genius, the
wealth, the commerce, the literatures, the government, and even the fashions of the modern
world.　　Here also, on this lake, the feudal
system, which was both the body and soul of the
Gallic effort in America, and whose ambition
was nothing less than entire possession of the
country from the Atlantic coast to the Rocky
Mountains, and from the Southern to the
Northern Gulf, after a century of struggle and
intrigue, and a dozen bloody campaigns, found
its Waterloo. Nominally, the conflict was closed
at Quebec, — and the death of Wolfe and Montcalm both on that fatal field of Abraham
Martin, outside the walls of the citadel, naturally and properly gave to that brief engage-
ment between a few hundred men a historic

brilliancy which fixes the gaze of all eyes upon its flashing splendor. But the great French leader knew well the truth and told it plainly when, a year and more before he fought his final battle, he warned the French monarch and his minister of war that the only hope for France to keep her hold upon the continent was to maintain her grip on Lake Champlain. And when the flag of France was lowered, at Amherst's resistless advance, at Ticonderoga, and Crown Point, it was then decided that the American continent was to be the home of an English Protestant civilization, and not the seat of a Papal-Gallic power. And if the student of American nationality would know the facts of its history, he must not begin with the feeble skirmish at Lexington, or the fierce disorderly fight on Bunker Hill, but come to this lake, for on it and its shores he will easily discover that Bunker Hill would never have been fought by the men whose fierce courage and knowledge of arms made it historic, had they not learned the deadly use of weapons, the value of discipline, and been nurtured in martial spirit by the warlike culture they received under the most skilful

and bravest generals of fighting England, in
their campaigns, battles, and forays against the
French and Indians here in the valley of Champlain.

In what school was Schuyler of New York
trained? Where did Putnam of Connecticut
learn to fight? Where did the grit of Stark of
New Hampshire get its razor edge? Whence
came the cannon that manned the works of
Washington on Dorchester heights and enabled
him to drive the British out of Boston? Fighting
against whom and where did New England and
New York men learn the use of arms, the habits
of obedience, the coolness of veterans under fire,
and that indifference to numbers which more
than once held the Revolutionary army together
and made it formidable to its foe? Here it
was, here on Lake Champlain and its connecting
waters, that the men who fought so bravely under
Prescott, Putnam, Stark, Gates, and Washington
learned the lesson of war and from it, as a martial school, graduated as veterans for the Revolutionary struggle. Is it not a most strange
thing that although nearly three centuries have
passed since the curtain was lifted and the first

act of a drama to which a hemisphere supplied
the audience and in whose successive scenes the
most ambitious kings, astute diplomats, famous
generals, the greatest financiers, and the most
dauntless spirits of Europe and England were
the actors, was played, there is not, with the
exception of Mr. Parkman's little silhouette of
the subject — a single page of accurate history
written?   A hundred and thirty-two years even
have come and gone since off the southeast
point of Valcour Island the last French flag
that waved about the waters of Champlain was
lowered, but American scholarship has in all
these years made no effort to collect the preg-
nant and impressive facts connected with the
French occupation of the lake, or prevent those
precious facts from drifting on the slow but
ever-moving current of time into oblivion.

CHAMPLAIN.

It was then, as the last of a long line of
glorious predecessors, that Champlain came
seeking, as all before him had done, the Northwest passage.   None braver than he had ever
gone before him.   Twenty times did he cross

the Atlantic — once in a shallop of sixteen tons
and once in one of barely twelve. Verily, he
was a sailor of whom the bravest of the old
mariners who had preceded him need not be
ashamed. In this mercenary age it were hard
to make men understand the motive which held
him to his performance amid perils numberless
and incredible labors. For he was not animated by the love of gold. Wealth he never
sought. He was not ambitious of lands and
feudal sovereignties, nor, so far as we can judge,
was he even ever emulous of fame. His was
the adventurous spirit, the seeking soul, the
searching mind, the eye eager to see new sights,
the ear that longed to hear strange sounds, and
the heart that craved to feel those fresh emotions which belong to the child-world and the
child-man. There was within him a rage for
knowledge. To see the waters of hitherto unseen seas; to inhale the wild odors of savage
woods, never breathed by man; to stand upon
the summits of untrodden mountains; to hear
the plunge of mighty waterfalls deeply hidden
in the enveloping forests; to behold the glories
of sunrises and of sunsets such as dwellers in

cities never see; to experience the unusual, the extraordinary, and the marvellous; in short, an unquenchable thirst for discovery was the animating motive in the bosom of Champlain. He was neither warrior, nor missionary, nor trader, nor scientist. His inspiration was not of the sword nor of the cross. Wealth he contemplated with indifferent eyes. To found a family or establish an empire he never dreamed. But to sail, to see, to hear, to feel, to know the joy of knowing what others knew not and of feeling what others never felt — this to Samuel Champlain was life.

CHAMPLAIN'S ENTRANCE INTO THE LAKE.

It was the 3d of July, 1609, when Champlain first gazed upon the lake which subsequently bore his name, and which to-day is the sole monument that perpetuates his fame. We do not know certainly the exact hour, but it was early in the morning when the canoe which bore him glided out from between the overhanging maples and cedars which lined either bank of the Richelieu, and entered the broader waters of the lake. The spectacle which met

his eyes was one which brought exclamations of
astonishment from his mouth, and as his canoe
swept onward over the level water new beauties
and wider expanses of natural loveliness broke
upon his view. Even then he was a world-wide
traveller. He had visited Mexico, Vera Cruz,
and Panama. The luxuriant loveliness of the
tropics and the more sober beauties of semi-tropi-
cal regions were familiar to him. He had seen
the best that the continent of Europe had to
show. He had gazed upon the green meadows of
Acadia and the awful grandeurs of the Saguenay.
But never before had he looked upon a scene of
such picturesque beauty, and such varied loveliness, as this body of water presented to his
appreciative eyes as it lay revealed in the dewy
light of this warm July morning.

Not a breath was moving in the air. The
lake, between its widening shores, stretched
before him smooth as glass. Through it the
noiseless paddles moved the noiseless bark in
which he stood and gazed. Behind him came the
twenty-four canoes, silently following his silent
wake. The paddles rose and sank in perfect
unison. The ochred faces of the Indians and

their feathered scalp-locks showed brilliantly in the morning light. The air was odorous with the perfumes of gums and flowers. Here and there lilies starred the water whitely. Large fish leaped, splashed, and drove their sharpened wedge of motion along the level surface. Through the dewy air came the pure, sweet note of the hermit thrush. Far overhead the hunting eagle, sweeping round and round in watchful circles, came to a sudden stop, fluttered for a moment, and then, with rightly balanced poise, drove headlong downward into the lake. Ducks blackened the water for acres. The mother-does watched the playful fawns bounding along the sand. The lumbering moose waded laboriously shoreward, and on the marshy bank stood at gaze. Above, the sky was sapphire. Over the eastern mountains the sun showed redly. The mighty woods came to the water's edge, an unbroken mass of natural forest. The lake, to which he was to give his name while living, that was to be his everlasting monument when dead, welcomed his entrance between her shores with the finest expressions of her loveliness. Champlain had come to his own, and his own received him gladly.

Thus they passed slowly up the lake. The
time that it took to make the passage of the
lake from its outlet to the point at which they
fought their battle with the Iroquois proved
that the party not only moved without haste,
but that Champlain, according to his custom,
circumnavigated its islands and made a thor-
ough exploration of its shores. For he entered
it on the 3d of July, and it was the 29th
of the month, as he records, when, paddling
along in the night; his party ran against the
Iroquois. These twenty-six days gave him sufficient time to examine the lake carefully.
This he undoubtedly did. Champlain was not
only a soldier and a navigator, but he was a
sportsman as well, a tourist. and a poet. He
loved nature for nature's sake. He did not
enter this lake to seek gold or foes. He was
seeking the Northwest passage, and a great
water-course to the west. Strange as such an
idea seems to us, it was a living reality to him,
as it had been to all the old mariners before him.
Both as a lover of nature and as an explorer,
bent on his romantic search, he would naturally
move slowly through the great water-course

which, passing out from the mouth of the Richelieu, he saw suddenly in long and glorious perspectives before him.

For Champlain was then as now a lake of
wide expanses and magnificent distances. It is
not walled into trough-like proportions as is
Memphremagog, nor has it the interruptions or
tame appearances of Mooshead, nor is it
smothered between monstrous mountains so
that its borders straighten and oppress it, as is
the case with the Horicon. But it is long and
wide and spacious. The eye ranges along perspectives that a hundred miles do not measure,
and the vistas which stretch before the gazer,
whether of water or of land, terminate in the
vagueness and dimness of distance. Lake
Champlain is not a lake that can be seen in a
day or in a week. and when we read in Champlain's record that he was twenty-six days in
making the distance between the outlet and the
southernmost point of his exploration, near
Ticonderoga, we know, instinctively, how the
days were filled with labors and with pleasures.
For neither in Nova Scotia nor on the banks of
the St. Lawrence from Labrador to Lachine, had

he ever found such sport as the waters, the
islands, and the shores of this lake gave him.
In his journal he records with amazement the
quantity and size of the fish which filled the
waters of the lake and the streams flowing into
it. And he was not a man to deny himself the
pleasures of the rod or of the gun when game
was plenty and the hunger of many justified the
sportsman's privilege. For twenty-six days he
shot and fished to his heart's content, circumnavigated the islands, explored the shores, ex-
amined the forests, and penetrated the rivers in
search of pleasure and of knowledge. Then suddenly his habit changed. His fishing and his
hunting ceased, and the explorer and sportsman
became a warrior. For, from what is now Apple-
tree Point or the northern shore of Burlington
Bay, the Algonquin chiefs pointed out to him the
significant shaft of "Mohawk Rock," and told
him that when they passed beyond its line they
were within the country of the terrible Iroquois
and must look to their caution and their courage for preservation. Champlain's gala day
was passed, and he was now drawing nigh to the
saddest day for him and France that either ever

knew; the day when he should shed blood
without cause. The blood of that United People, the strongest and most warlike confederacy
of Red men on the continent, and of whom
the fame was as wide as their sovereignty, that
they never forgot a friend or forgave a foe.
Strange fate this which befell the just and
humane Champlain; that, stumbling on, in his
ignorance of Indian politics and power, he
should, by one blundering shot, on the shores of
this lake that was to bear his name, decide the
character of a civilization, and forfeit a continent to France.

The picture of the battle between Champlain
and his allies and the Iroquois is thus drawn by
himself : —

"BATTLE WITH THE IROQUOIS.

"At nightfall we embarked in our canoes,
and as we were advancing noiselessly onward
we encountered a war party of Iroquois at the
point of a cape which juts into the lake on the
west side. It was on the 29th of the month
and about ten o'clock at night. They and we
began to shout, seizing our arms. We with-

drew to the water, and the Iroquois paddled to the shore, arranged their canoes, and began to hew down trees with villainous-looking axes and fortified themselves very securely. Our party kept their canoes one alongside of the other, tied to poles, so as not to run adrift, in order to fight all together if need be. When everything was arranged they sent two canoes to know if their enemies wished to fight. They answered that they desired nothing else, but that there was not then light enough to distinguish each other and that they would fight at sunrise. This was agreed to. On both sides the night was spent in dancing and singing, mingled with insults and taunts. Thus they sung, danced, and insulted each other until day broke. My companions and I were concealed in separate canoes belonging to the savage Montagnais. After being equipped with light armor, each of us took an arquebus and went ashore. I saw the enemy leaving their barricade. They were about two hundred men, strong and robust, who were coming toward us with a gravity and assurance that greatly pleased me, led on by three chiefs. Ours were marching in similar order, who told me that those who bore the three lofty plumes were the chiefs and that I must do all I could to kill them. I promised to do the best I could. The moment we landed they began to run toward the enemy, who stood firm and had not yet perceived my companions, who went into the bush with some savages. Ours commenced calling on me with a loud voice, opening way for me and placing me at their head, about twenty paces in advance, until I was about thirty paces from the enemy. The moment they saw me they halted, gazing at me and I at them. When I saw them preparing to shoot at us, I raised my arquebus, and, aiming directly at one of the chiefs, two of them fell to the ground by this shot, and one of their companions received a wound of which he died afterwards. I had put four balls in my arquebus. Ours, on witnessing a shot so favorable to them, set up such tremendous shouts that thunder could not have been heard, and yet there was no lack of arrows on one side or the other. The Iroquois were greatly astonished at seeing two men killed so instantaneously, notwithstanding that they were provided with arrow-proof armor woven of cotton thread and wood. This frightened them very much.

"Whilst I was reloading, one of my companions fired a shot, which so astonished them anew, seeing their chiefs slain, that they lost courage, took to flight, and abandoned the field and their fort, hiding in the depths of the forest, whither pursuing them, I killed some others. Our savages also killed several of them and took ten or twelve of them prisoners. The rest carried off the wounded. Fifteen or sixteen of ours were wounded. These were promptly treated.

"After having gained this victory, our party amused themselves plundering Indian corn and meal from the enemy, and also their arms, which they had thrown away the better to run. And having feasted, danced, and sung, we returned three hours afterwards with the prisoners."

Such is Champlain's description of the battle. As to the exact locality of the fight there has been much learned (?) dispute. To my own mind there can be no doubt as to it. The place was nigh Ticonderoga. Champlain distinctly marks the locality on his map of the lake: that is enough to settle it. On their return trip, Champlain was compelled to be a spectator of one of those appalling scenes incident to Indian warfare, — the torture of a prisoner. It undoubtedly took place at Willsboro' Point, near where the hotel now stands. Champlain strove in vain to save the victim from the torture, and to deliver him from prolonged agonies; and, finally, in mercy, shot him dead at the stake.

It was in this encounter that the Aquanu Schioni — United People, as the confederated Indians called themselves — saw for the first time a Christian white man, and were taught their first lesson in the humane ethics of what is called Christianity. It was in this battle also that the red warriors of the Mohawk had their first introduction to a Frenchman. For a hundred and fifty years they carried the memory of it on the edge of their tomahawks and the points of their scalping-knives. More than once the recollection of the wrong done them on the shore of Champlain by the armed representative of Old France, of the blood of their chiefs there ruthlessly shed, stood like a wall of fire between the feeble English settlement south of them and the French and Indian hordes which were marshalled to destroy them in the north. More than once France, through Church and State, practised all the arts of persuasion and intimidation to entice the dreaded Iroquois to her side or wedge them from their alliance with the English, and failed. They could not forget what France had done to them in their first encounter near Ticonderoga. The slaughter of the Indian chiefs by Champlain was not only a crime but a political blunder — a blunder of such magnitude and so far-reaching in its after results as to become monumental. As it needs but a single stone dropped into the feeble current at its source to decide in which direction a river shall flow — whether toward the south or toward the north — so it needs but one act by one of the participants at the beginning of the course of events to decide what, years after, shall be the character of the results and final outcome of them. If Champlain could have foreseen what his slaughterous shots had done for France that morning; could he but have heard the yells of hate, the screams of agony, the shrieks of torture which were to rise for a hundred years as awful echoes to his fatal gun, he would then and there have turned his arquebus against himself and expiated with his own life his crime against France and humanity. It has been said that long before he died he realized both his sin and his blunder, and with sincere contrition bemoaned the one and deplored the other. But on the day the crime was done and blunder committed he did neither. For after the battle was over and the tumult had died away, flushed with victory, standing on the shore of the lake with the vision of its loveliness stretching onward before him, he joyfully claimed it for France and named it with his own name.

The student can but be impressed with the good-fortune that attended Champlain in his life and remained faithful to his memory after death. In this respect he stands in sharp contrast with that throng of adventurous spirits whose courage and whose toils were equal to his own, but who, in life and death, missed his happy fortunes.

De Soto sleeps in a nameless grave on the bank of the river he discovered but could not name. Sir Humphrey Gilbert perished on a tempestuous night in mid-ocean. His grave is a sailor's grave, without name and without spot. John Cabot gave to England a continent, and not an English-speaking man knows where he is buried. Leif Erickson discovered America four hundred years before Columbus was born, and the fame of the great deed has been given to another. Sir Hugh Willoughby found death and forgetfulness in an unknown Lapland harbor. Henry Hudson was turned adrift from his ship by his mutinous crew in the midst of the bay that bears his name, and at the prime of life, with his little son, drifted to an unknown death. La Salle, the noblest spirit after Champlain, and the most daring soul old France ever sent westward, sleeps where he was murdered under the verbenas of an unknown Texan prairie. Verendrye, first of white men to see the summits of the Rocky Mountains, slumbers tombless. Jogues, the priest, first of his race to see the Horicon, was tomahawked in a Mohawk village, while the name he gave to the lake has been

shoved aside for that of the coarse Hanoverian
King.   What strange fortunes befell these old-
time wanderers who explored the world, who
gave islands and continents to civilization, who
by their exploits clomb to the highest levels of
fame, and who were thus pursued by an ironical
fate even after they had passed through the port-
als of death !   For, of them all, Champlain left,
in dying, to the clear knowledge of men who
were to come after, the two things they most
wish to know and visit — a grave and a monu-
.ment.   For, at Quebec the tourist and pilgrim
can see the spot where his body sleeps, and in
the lake that bears his name they can behold a
monument as magnificent and enduring as his
fame.

MOHAWK ROCK.

In Burlington Bay there stands a rock.
Straight up from out the water it rises, bare of
soil and sharply pointed, a veritable interrogation point to puzzle the curious voyager. Has
it special geologic or historic significance, and, if
it has, who may tell its origin or declare its connection ? Is it the core of some island washed

away by the waves of ages; a geologic remnant
of ancient days, shrunken from fair and verdant
fulness to this bare spike of stone; or was it
shot upward by some terrific force which, long
pent, was suddenly let loose in throe or spasm of
Nature; a volcanic spear-point of stone darted
out of chaos when all her forces were hot in
maddest action?   Who will answer the dumb
interrogation of this strangely pointed stone, or
translate from the historic silences around and
above it messages of knowledge?

Men call it Rock Dunder, a meaningless name
gotten from a silly tradition, too silly to mention.   This is a monumental stone standing here
in Burlington Bay, a memorial shaft, older than
the column of Trajan, older than the Agora of the
Greeks.   The fame of this rock was continental.
Centuries upon centuries before the white man
came, it was known to every Indian warrior from
Cape Breton to Lake Erie, and from Labrador
to Florida.   Among all the Red Nations it was
known and named with awe.   It was a landmark
to half the continent, a landmark of nationality
and empire, a pillar of authority, a symbol of
sovereignty sustained by a thousand battles dur-

ing years innumerable. For, from Lake Huron running east even to this rock in Burlington Bay, came the boundary line between the Iroquois and Algonquin, the two great Indian races which held the continent east of the Mississippi, as modern men of different and hostile races hold their countries whose boundaries touch and which for either party to cross means war.

Of all the Indian tribes the confederated Five Nations were ever the most renowned. They were more civilized than the Greeks when Solon framed his code for his countrymen; they were as brave as the Greeks who fought at Thermopylæ. Their chiefs loved battle like the old Norse Vikings. The Everglades of Florida paid them tribute, and the Esquimaux of Labrador had felt the weight of their tomahawks. The tribes of the Mississippi acknowledged their sovereignty, and the nations that camped round the shores of Lake St. John kept their sentinels pushed well southward in dread of their fierce invasion. But of the Five Nations, each fierce as a hunting eagle, the Mohawks stood in war pre-eminent, unmatched, and invincible.

What of this? Much. This rock in Burlington Bay, in that former time, was Mohawk Rock; the landmark of their northern boundary; their mute and savage challenge to all the great tribes of the North, to come beyond it southward if they dared. It is not known what they called it in their tongue; the old writings spell it differently and give it different interpretations. I care nothing for them, for it is plain that all speak of it out of their ignorance. Of it all, only one thing is certain, which is that this pointed spire of stone in Burlington Bay was known to the Indians of half the continent as Mohawk Rock, and that it marked the northern point of their savage power and fierce dominion.

To this rock they came to declare war or peace with all the other tribes. Around it they gathered in their war canoes for fierce invasions northward. From this mute rock they fought their way into the Huron country, until they held in their firm grasp Hochelaga, now Montreal. North of this bare rock the Mohawk might go as far as his bravery could carry him, but south of this great national sign no Huron

might ever come one step and live.   Away, then,
with the silly name that local ignorance has
given to this historic stone, this monument of
ancient times, old with unnumbered centuries
when Champlain came, and give back to it that
significant and noble name by which the Red
races knew it, when by them it was, in peace
and war, treaty and tribute, mentioned, in honor
or in fear, as " Mohawk Rock."

There are localities in the world which, when
visited, provoke the imagination.   There are
spots from which the fancy of man with free
wing starts for flight as naturally as a waking
bird from his morning perch.   I have visited
such localities and felt their influence upon me.
I have gone as pilgrim to such places, and from
their altitude gazing backward beheld the martial pomp and glory of departed days.   What
might not this old stone tell us if it might speak
of old-time wars and peace, of treaties made and
broken by the old-time warriors who gathered in
solemn councils within sight of it, feasted their
friends and tortured their captive foes beneath
the mighty pines which lined in those far days
with a forest wall the shores of Burlington Bay ?

Some night, if you have imagination, when the lake sleeps, and through the dusk the lights of heaven shine dimly, paddle out across the still water, climb this ancient rock, and, sitting upon the crest of it, listen to the silence brooding around you; that silence which is not empty but full of knowledge and understanding of what it has seen and heard. Make your mood receptive, and, it may be, you will see and hear many things, — the low murmur of solemn council, the battle chant, the orator's appeal, the signal for assault, the dying yell, the tortured victim's moan, the funeral lament. Nor shall your eyes lack sights that will enlarge them; for onward through the gloom in long lines with measured paddle stroke you will see canoes of war come on, pass you, and disappear sweeping northward; and all around the shores where now the city stands, your eyes will see a great wood of pines, lighted up with a thousand fires so that each trunk stands forth like a dark brown pillar, and, in the wood thus lighted, you will behold hundreds upon hundreds of warriors, ochred for battle, passing to and fro. And with this vision of aboriginal life and times standing vividly outlined in person and circumstance before you, you will realize what so few learn, that to him who has knowledge and imagination both there is no hidden past. The thing which puzzles us is not the past but the future; not the door which has been shut, but that strange door which has never been opened. For who, although knocking with reddened knuckles against it, may start even an echo? The lost past we can reconquer, but the future, who may invade it, or who, of it, may tell us one single thing?

TICONDEROGA.

I do not propose to write the history of the rocky bluff which lies between the waters of Lake Champlain and the outlet of the Horicon. Lacking the proportions and grandeur of Cape Diamond at Quebec, it nevertheless matches it in historic significance. If Quebec was the head, Ticonderoga and Crown Point were the two mailed hands of the French power, and, with these two hands, until they were severed from her body, France held the country firmly in her grasp. In the surrender of Quebec the colonial

effort of France on this continent expired. Its
last breath was breathed with the dying gasp of
Montcalm, but it received its death-blow at
Ticonderoga. There it was that the steel of
England, directed by the skill of Pitt and driven
home by the conqueror of Louisburg, reached
its vitals. From Ticonderoga she staggered
toward Quebec as a wounded bear drags herself
to her den, not in hopes of escaping death, but
that she may make, at its mouth, one more and
her last fight for her cubs.

The aborigines called the stony promontory
Cheonderoga, or the place of many and mellow
sounds, in reference to the dull roar of the falls,
and the soft sounds of the rushing rapids that
filled the smothering woods with mellow noise
as the clear waters of the Horicon tumbled or
rushed over their obstructions a mile beyond.

The French, acknowledging the poetic justice
of the name, called it Carillon, — the Place of
Chimes, — and year after year the soldiers of
France within the fortress listened to the
cadence of the falling waters of summer nights
and fancied that they heard the church chimes
of their native land. It is a wonder that the

stolid English who drove out the French did not rechristen it Camel's Neck, or that the vulgarizing American settlers who succeeded the Briton did not stigmatize it as Hog Point. But, protected by some rare fortune or the Genius of the place, to whose unknown name we offer our grateful acknowledgments, it still retains its old Indian name, with a slight alteration in its spelling.

The fortress whose ruins the tourist may still see and explore was built by the French in 1756. And to the student of history and the traveller alike they are the most interesting ones on the continent. The fortress was surrounded by water on three sides, and a portion of the remaining side was a dense swamp. This landward side was defended by a breastwork nine feet in height and a thick abattis of fallen trees whose branches were sharpened to a point. This abattis was six rods deep along the entire breastwork, and dense, and constituted a horrible tangle of impenetrable obstruction. Against this breastwork, protected by its frightful abattis, the incompetent Abercrombie sent, time and again, in vain and successive charges, the finest regiments of England and the colonies. For four hours the unequal and awful contest lasted, and when at last the signal to retire was sounded and the maddened but exhausted soldiery drew back from the gory spot, two thousand bodies were left in that awful parallelogram—twenty-three rods long by eight rods wide—to emphasize the incompetency of English generalship, and French skill and courage. It was the bloodiest battle ever fought on land before or since upon the continent, as the naval battle off Plattsburgh was the bloodiest battle ever fought on any water known to history.

The next year, General Amherst conquered the fortress with little, if any, loss. But Montcalm, Levis, Boulamaque and the white-coated troops that loved the battle with them were not there, or the victor of Louisburg would have won it by skill if he won it at all, rather than by bravery. For England never had a commander on this continent that might be compared with Montcalm, unless his companion in death—the gifted but delicate Wolfe—might be called his peer.

One summer night I visited this most historic of all our historic places, this most romantic of all our ruins, and watched the night out seated upon its crumbled walls or wandering along its mounded ramparts. The moon was at its full, and its white ghostly light gave fitting illumination to the spot where so many in other years had fought and died. I doubt if any, even the dullest, might be so placed and not have both memory and imagination quickened. As for myself, I will confess that night and its emotions remain after a quarter of a century of time as clearly and impressively engraved on my memory as the features of my mother's face. To me as to the red men Ticonderoga was a name of nature, suggestive of mellow sounds, for to my ears, through the damp air of dewy upland and foggy river, there came the murmur of rapids and the voices of the waters of the falls mellowed by the distance. Then came the memory of later times, — of war and battles, — and I heard the measured fall of sentinel feet; the hourly call from angle unto angle; and caught the gleam of cannon on the ramparts and of stacked arms and long lines of blanketed forms sleeping on the warm turf beyond the glacis. Below me on the pallid water I saw canoes come noiselessly out of distance and into distance go as noiselessly. To the angle of the wall nigh where I sat Montcalm came and on it seated himself. Soon De Levis joined him, then Boulamaque with Bourgansville. And last of all Marin, the scout, the only rival in skill and courage that Rogers and Putnam ever had, and who saved the latter from the stake,[1] even when the fagots were on fire around him. Together in low tones they talked of France and loved ones; of battles fought and won; of comrades dead or distant; of perils passed and

---

[1] Putnam, while scouting, was taken a prisoner by some of Marin's command. They bound him to a tree and one of the Indians amused himself by seeing how near he could throw his tomahawk to the prisoner's head without touching it. Putnam bore the ordeal unflinchingly, and at the close of it a Canadian put his fusee at Putnam's breast and snapped it. Fortunately it missed fire, at which the scoundrel gave him a severe blow in the face with the butt end of his gun. Putnam was then taken to the spot where the Indians were encamped, and his clothes stripped from him. They then bound him to a tree, piled a great brush heap around him, and set it on fire. It was at this moment, when the flames were penetrating through the brush toward his body, that his great rival and foe, with whom he had fought a hundred skirmishes, — Marin, — burst through the throng of Indians, scattered the burning brushes and brands, and cut the withes that bound Putnam to the stake with his knife.

perils yet to come. Then round them gathered their great foes: Lord Howe — who in the field matched the younger Pitt in the cabinet, whose virtues made him envied of death, over whose lifeless form the rough Putnam sobbed like a girl, and the largest army England ever marshalled in America stood appalled at its loss: Abercrombie, the incompetent, to whom Montcalm lifted his chapeau in derision; Amherst, cautious, persistent, brave, with the laurels of Louisburg on his brow; Campbell of Invernwe, mysteriously fated unto death; Rogers, the great scout — the only scout of fame, who after Lexington loved the King of England better than his country; Arnold, Townshend, Lyman, Johnson, Montgomery, Gates, Ethan Allen, Seth Warner, Remember Baker, Stark, and Putnam — all came as to a familiar place and stood before me making such a group of fame, as history cannot equal at any other citadel or ancient battle plain save one — Quebec.

Then came the dawn and with it the rush of feet, the sharp click of a firelock at the postern, and the stentorian voice of Ethan Allen demanding of Laplace that the fortress be surren-

dered to him, speaking " in the name of
Jehovah and the Continental Congress." [1]

With such recollections and musings was my
mind filled as I sat or wandered amid the ruins
of Ticonderoga on that moon-lighted summer
night, until with the hours of it moving in con-
cert, the dim stars passed from sight, and over
the mountains of the east the sun rose resplen-
dently strong and bright, lighting with his
rays a great and prosperous land whose liberty
and religion owe so much to Ticonderoga,

[1] The following address was delivered by Ethan Allen to his
eighty-three compatriots as they stood on the western shore of the
lake, after they had been ferried across ready to make their desperate attempt to capture the fortress. The date was May 10,
1775, and the hour was that of early dawn. I preserve the words
of the address, as illustrative of the bravery of the leader and the
led.

" Friends and fellow-soldiers, you have for years past been a
scourge and a terror to arbitrary power. Your valor has been
famed abroad and acknowledged, as appears by the advice and
orders to me from the General Assembly of Connecticut to surprise and take the garrison now before us. I propose to advance
before you and in person conduct you through the wicket gate; for
we must this morning either quit our pretensions to valor or possess ourselves of this fortress in a few minutes; and inasmuch
as it is a desperate attempt, which none but the bravest of men
dare undertake, I do not urge it on any contrary to his will.
You who will undertake it with me voluntarily *poise your
firelocks*."

Allen relates that every man did poise his firearm.

whose ruins still stand to remind every citizen of the Great Republic of their everlasting debt.

CROWN POINT.

Next to Ticonderoga in interest to the student of American history, and in some respects superior to it, stands Crown Point and the region around about it. Geographically it is in truth *The Gate of the Lake*, for such is the narrowness of the lake at this point that the feeblest of armaments might close it to all passage. The French early perceived the importance of this peculiarity of its topography from a military point of view, and built a fort there as early as 1731.[1] It was 1759 when, at the

[1] The fortress which the French built in 1731 was called Fort St. Frederic, and was so utterly destroyed by them when they evacuated it in 1759, that, on the arrival of General Amherst's command, he found only blackened walls and ruined passages. It was because of the blackened chimneys of the burned houses that were left standing amid the surrounding ruins that the locality received the name of "Chimney Point," a name by which it is still known.

Amherst immediately traced out the lines of a new fort some forty rods west of the site of the old Fort St. Frederic. He planned a magnificent fortification. The ramparts were twenty-five feet thick, over twenty feet in height and of solid masonry. The cur-

victorious advance of Amherst, they left it forever. For more than a hundred years the
banner of France had waved above the walls of
the fortress that French power had erected, and
held in evidence that Lake Champlain and its
shores belonged to it.

It is a strange fact that historically Crown
Point is a mystery and a puzzle. There are
many evidences that at some unknown period
it was the centre of a large population. Proofs
of a populous and permanent occupation are
not wanting. It is evident even now that the
shores of Bulwagga Bay, for many rods, at
places, were, at some remote period, graded and
artificially sloped to the water. Signs of
ancient fences and enclosures as of gardens
and door-yards may still be seen. In some of
these enclosures aged fruit trees, of whose plant-
ing none living knew, were standing within the
recollection of present owners. There is an

tains were from fifty to one hundred yards in length, and the circuit of the ramparts measured over eight hundred yards. A deep
and wide ditch hewn from the solid rock surrounded the entire
work. It was never completed, although what was done on it cost
the English government over ten millions of dollars. It is this
work, undertaken by Amherst in 1759, the ruins of which are now
visible to the tourist.

old street that can be traced, made of broken
stone like the macadamized roads of to-day.
Ancient cellars, some of them hewn from the
solid rock, still line this street. There is a
sidewalk made of flagging still to be seen, but
none can tell who laid it. These stones are
worn, and show that they have been pressed by
countless feet. There are, moreover, two large
graveyards, —

"Great cities filled with pale inhabitants,"

which tell that hundreds and thousands who
lived, loved, and labored once were here.

Settlers who came in to settle the country
after the Revolution said that they found a
large tract, miles in extent, with not a tree or
bush on it, that had evidently been highly cultivated. In these same fields, now largely over-
grown with a heavy forest, asparagus, herbs,
and bushes usually cultivated by man can still
be seen. Rogers, the famous scout, in one of
his letters, speaks of wide fields around Crown
Point, and that they were covered with noble
crops. He also writes of settlements on the
east side of the lake, and of "three hundred

men, chiefly inhabitants of the adjacent villages." But if there were "three hundred
men" in these villages, then the total population on the *east* side of the lake, within sight of
the fort, must have been at least fifteen hundred. How many, then, were probably on the
west side, where the real centre and power, the
military possession and commerce, were? Kalm,
the Swedish traveller, said that "about the fort
in 1749 were a large settlement, and pleasant
cultivated fields and gardens." There is no
doubt that Crown Point was at one time not
only the centre of a vast aboriginal traffic in
skins and peltries, but also of a large commercial exchange between the French and Dutch
and English settlements of which we have no
record. My own belief is that at one time
the population of Crown Point was not less
than five thousand souls. Any intelligent
tourist will find this locality a most interesting
one to visit and examine.

The campaign of 1759, under the command
of Amherst, secured the possession of the continent to England. The French left Crown
Point, as they had a few days before left Ticon-

deroga, on his approach forever, and Amherst at once set to work to erect an impregnable and magnificent fortress. The ruins of this work still bear witness to its original strength and splendor. With those at Ticonderoga they compose the most extensive and impressive ruins erected by white men on the continent. The trenches and ramparts can still be clearly traced. The barracks still remain in part. The great bakery is well preserved. The old fireplaces are to be seen, and on the walls names and scribblings traced by hands that have been powerless to hold pen or knife for a hundred years. The last time I visited the site of old Fort Frederick at Crown Point, sheep were feeding on the grassy rampart, and a phœbe was singing her liquid note at the mouth of the old magazine.

ARNOLD'S BATTLE AT VALCOUR ISLAND.

We are not an admirer of Benedict Arnold, considered in the light of a military commander only, and wholly apart from the dastard act which made him infamous as a traitor to his country. Nor can we find in his career as a commander in his various undertakings any justification of the honorable place which historians have awarded him. For, so far as we are aware, he never won a victory or accomplished anything of practical value to the cause that he served for years with undoubted personal courage. That he was brave in battle and energetic in preparation is true, but the same might be claimed for hundreds and thousands to whom fame was never awarded, and in whose behalf no claim of it might, with any show of reason, be advanced. If success is in warlike undertakings the proper gauge of merit, the court from whose decision no appeal can be taken, then Benedict Arnold was never deserving of especial honor or honorable mention in history, for success never attended his efforts.

Judged by his record, if he was a hero at all, he was a hero of failures. Offensively egotistic and vain, envious and revengeful to a degree, mean and dishonest, a boaster and a liar, he deserved condemnation and contempt for the meanness of his personal traits and innumerable acts of injustice long before the inherent wickedness of his nature and the growing sinfulness of his career culminated in his betrayal of his country. His battle at Valcour was not only a defeat, but a defeat that might have been avoided.

It was the middle of August when he took command of his fleet at Crown Point. It was respectable in the number of its vessels and their armament. It was re-enforced before the 11th of October, when he fought the battle at Valcour, until it carried over eighty guns and seven hundred men. At Ticonderoga and Crown Point General Gates had an army of nearly ten thousand troops. They were in a good state of discipline, and efficiently armed. Crown Point was then, as it had been for a hundred years, the key to the position. Behind its batteries Arnold could, at any time, if pushed by the English, have found safety for his fleet. Wisdom required, nay, demanded, that he should fight the English — when he fought them — in the open lake, so that in case of defeat he might retire behind the guns of Crown Point, or even, if necessary, above the protecting works at Ticonderoga. This plan he was urged to adopt by Waterbury and other captains of his ships.

Why he did not adopt it is explainable only on the ground of his complete incompetency to command in a large undertaking. What he did do was to place his whole fleet — which he knew was inferior to that of his antagonist — in such a position that it could not fight save at close quarters, and, in case of defeat, could not retire in safety or together. The result was that his men fought bravely and his fleet was destroyed.

Valcour Island lies on the western side of the lake, several miles below Cumberland Head. Between it and the shore there is half a mile of water. The entrance to this passage between the island and shore is wider from the south than from the north. Allowing that the English fleet would attack him from the south — which it did — he would, in case he was defeated, be entirely cut off from the line of retreat, and have no resort save the negligence of the victors or sheer luck. This was all pointed out to him by his captains, but he gave them no heed. He anchored his fleet in a line from Valcour to the shore and waited the coming of Pringle!

It was October 11, and at eight o'clock of the morning, when the English fleet were discovered off Cumberland Head. The wind was blowing freshly from the north, and before it the fleet, with swelling canvas, was booming rapidly along. Past Valcour, a mile to the east of it, they swept, every glass directed and every eye gazing southward, expecting that Arnold would be discovered far up the lake. Imagine their surprise when, suddenly, they saw his whole fleet bunched inside of Valcour! A glance revealed its inferiority to their own, and the certainty of their victory. It was reported that the English commander, as he wore his ship around toward the west, took a long look at Arnold's position through his glass, and exclaimed to General Carlton, who was standing by his side: "What a brave fool he is!" An accurate description!

There is no need to describe the battle. The Americans fought with courage, of course. Arnold did the work of a common gunner, pointing nearly every piece on the Congress himself. Waterbury, on the Washington, fought his ship like a commander, from the quarter-deck, and at the close of the conflict was the only active officer on board. It was Water-

bury who had been most insistent that the fleet
should make its fight on the open water of the
lake and from the south of the enemy. Even
after the English appeared off Cumberland Head,
it is recorded that he went on board the Congress, and urged Arnold to get under way and
run the fleet out from the pot-hole where it was
anchored. The battle was fought and won by
the English gunboats only and one schooner.
The Thunderer, the Loyal Convert, the Inflexi-
ble, and the larger vessels of the English took
no part in the action. Pringle had been unable
to bring them up to windward in time. They
were not needed. The defeat of Arnold was
complete, and would have been ignominious but
for the courage of his captains and the bravery
of his men. The only vessels that succeeded in
reaching Crown Point were one sloop, one
schooner, a gondola, and a galley. No wonder
that the principal officers of his fleet called him
"The Evil Genius of the North." He should
have been cashiered and dismissed from service in disgrace. But General Gates, for some
unaccountable reason, covered up the facts
of the case in his report to Congress, and

thus enabled the most incompetent of commanders to become the worst of traitors to his country.[1]

[1] It seems proper that the following incident, illustrative of the "cruelty of the savage," as it is well accredited, should be preserved. While the fight was being hotly contested, a Mrs. Hay. who lived in a house on the mainland near the scene of the conflict, carrying her infant in her arms, went to a spring near the lake which flowed through a dense thicket. To her horror she suddenly found herself in the midst of a large force of Indians, terrible in their war paint, and all armed with guns and tomahawks. She, realizing her peril, clasped her babe to her bosom, and burst into tears. An aged chief approached her, and, unable to console her in her own language, gently wiped her tears from her cheeks with the soft fringe of his hunting shirt, and then motioned her to return to her house, where she remained unmolested. This is only a typical case of the treatment which white women received at the hands of the red Indian, whom the historian Parkman goes out of his way — whenever he can find the least excuse — to revile and malign. I have heard a thoroughly informed student of our Indian wars publicly assert that there was not a single instance in our history of a white woman having been outraged or insulted by a pure-blooded Indian, nor of one being tortured as a captive, no matter how bitterly she may have fought them, and only a few cases of white women being killed, even in the moments of their wildest rage. If Mr. Parkman will recall the *ordinary* treatment which maidens and matrons alike received at the hands of the *Christian* and *civilized* soldiery of Europe when a city was captured and sacked; if he will recall the unnamable tortures which were inflicted by *priestly* exemplars of the mercies of God in Peru; or the horrible mutilations and agonizing deaths inflicted on the Waldenses and Huguenots by the sanction or order of the Vice-gerent of God on earth — the recollection might, perhaps, make him more fair and scholarly in his indictment of the Indian race.

MACDONOUGH'S VICTORY IN PLATTSBURG'S BAY.

The battle between the American and English fleet off Plattsburg, Sept. 11, 1813, was one which can be recalled with pride by the countrymen of those who won and those who lost; for the fight was one of the most desperate ever fought in ships, and from first to last the contest was waged by either party with equal skill and courage. The same blood was in either host, and the same grim, stubborn way of fighting characterized the ships that bore the Stars and the ships that bore the Cross. The armaments were nearly the same in number and calibre of their guns and in the force of fighting men engaged, while the commandants of the hostile fleets were men of tried skill and courage, and the captains under them were of that metal whose edge loved the fierce friction of the fray and sharpened to it as it raged on.

The conditions which preceded and attended the conflict were rare and rarely perfect. Each fleet was built in expectation of it and under the eye of the admiral who was to bring it into

action. Macdonough was of fighting stock
and fame, and at Vergennes had built his vessels and armed them for this fight. Downie
knew well whom and what sort of a man he
was to meet, and had prepared a perfect equip-
ment for the desperate meeting wisely and well.
Each knew that the fight was to be on level
water and within pistol range, where every
shot would tell, and that the perfection of
armament and the skill and courage with which
the guns were served would decide the issue.
Each knew that when it came it would be a
duel — a duel to the death ; and that grit — the
grit of the most warlike blood of the world —
would settle it. Each knew also that two
armies drawn up in battle array on the nigh
shores, under the same banners which floated
over the two fleets, would supply the audience
fit for such a noble scene, while two nations
would wait in suspense for the first tidings of
the fray. Seldom, if ever, in the history of
naval warfare have such stimulating conditions
preceded and attended a contest between the
contestants.

It was eight o'clock of the morning when the

British vessels rounded Cumberland Head and got their first view of their foe, who lay in battle line awaiting them. Macdonough's arrangement of his ships was perfect. From near Crab Island his line stretched straight across the bay northward to a point abreast of Cumberland Head, but somewhat inside of it. At the head of the line was the Eagle, Captain Henly commander. The Eagle was a brig as to its rig, mounting twenty guns and manned with one hundred and fifty men. Next to her in order, toward the south, lay Macdonough with the flag-ship, the Saratoga, mounting twenty-six guns, with two hundred and twelve men. Then came the Ticonderoga, Cassin commanding, with seventeen guns and one hundred and ten men; and next in order, ending the line near Crab Island, was the Preble, Budd commanding, with seven guns and thirty men. She lay so near the shoal stretching northeastward from the island as to prevent the line from being turned by the enemy.

To the rear of the first line of battle thus placed were ten gunboats mounted with twenty-four, eighteen, and twelve pounders, and carrying some thirty-five men each, and so placed as to command the intervals between the vessels of the front line and able to support them in emergency. In this wise manner had Macdonough made his line of battle; and, standing on the high shore above Plattsburg, one can in imagination see to-day his fleet lying ready for action.

Macdonough's spirit was of the highest, his mood heroic. A captain of one of his ships signalled to inquire if it would not be well to serve a ration of grog to the crews before the conflict opened — a custom universal in those days on fighting ships thus placed. He declined the suggestion and signalled back that his men should fight that fight braced by no other stimulant than their native courage and their patriotic love for their country. It has been said that his brave reply was received with cheers by the entire fleet. In this brave style and spirit, as the British bore up against them, the Americans stood silently and bravely at their guns, while the two hostile armies on the shore paused in their initial skirmishing, each regiment standing at rest to see the fight begin.

The English fleet was brought into action in
a manner worthy of the brave Downie's reputation and the best traditions of their naval service.   He bore up against the Saratoga, and
anchored within   two   cable-lengths without
firing a shot.   The Confiance was a frigate;
her armament thirty-seven guns, with a crew of
three hundred men.   There were many of her
officers and men who had fought under Nelson
at Trafalgar and knew how to fight a ship in
silence until she sunk.   Lying thus at shortest
range, on level water, abreast of the Saratoga,
she poured into her her broadside of twenty-
four-pounders with an explosion as of one gun.
The effect of the awful discharge was terrific.
Macdonough's ship shook from stem to stern as
the monstrous weight of plunging metal struck
her, and staggered like a man hit suddenly on
the breast by a giant's fist.   That one fearful
discharge disabled forty of her crew.

Thus was the battle opened, and for two
hours and a half, with the thunder of heated
guns, the crash of shattered wood, the shout
and cheers of men, the snapping of booms and
yards and masts, swathed from sight in sulphur-

ous smoke, the brave antagonists fought it out.
None flinched.   The brave Downie fell dead on
his deck.   Twice was Macdonough down.   Once
the head of a gunner, severed from his body,
was driven against him with such violence that
it knocked him into the scuppers.   No man was
called wounded in either fleet if he could keep
on his feet or pass ammunition on his knees.
Midshipman Lee of the Confiance said that he
doubted if there were five men out of the three
hundred that were not killed or wounded.   The
Saratoga was hulled fifty-five times and was
twice on fire.   The Confiance was hulled one
hundred and five times.   The Americans lost
one man in every eight, killed or wounded, and
at the close of the action there was not a mast
in either fleet fit for use.   In both fleets the
lower rigging hung down as if but just placed,
in setting up, over the mastheads.   The masts
themselves were so splintered that they looked
like bunches of matches, and the sails, tattered
and begrimed with powder, like bundles of old
rags.   Well-informed writers have said that it
was the bloodiest naval battle ever fought by a
fleet of ships.

The last time I passed over the historic water on which this dreadful battle was fought, it was in a yacht at whose peak, at equal height, the Red Cross of St. George and the Stars and Stripes waved in evidence of the friendship and affection which now exists between the two great nations which seventy-six years ago fought each other so fiercely in Plattsburg Bay.

FORT MONTGOMERY.

At the northern end of the lake, where it narrows into the river Richelieu, at the national boundary line, stands Fort Montgomery. It is a large fine military work of chiselled stones, each and every one being laid with the skill of finest masonry. It was begun in 1844, immediately upon the conclusion of the Webster-Ashburton Treaty, which moved our national line northward from Cumberland Head to the outlet of the lake, which gave us not only much valuable territory, but, in case of war with Great Britain or Canada, a strategic position absolutely beyond price. This fort is not completed, and never will be, I trust. We need no military works upon this continent along the line which divides the

northern from the southern half of it.
Whether Canadians or States men, we Americans are one in destiny. Our race characteristics, our commercial interests, our social customs, our political habits and ambitions are the same. Geographically, the American continent is a unit, and the great people who are to inhabit it for centuries to come must be a united people. Three hundred millions south of the St. Lawrence and thirty millions north of it are an impossibility. If in their ignorance or wilfulness the smaller section would not coalesce with the larger, it would surely and shortly be overborne, not by the force of arms, perhaps, but by the pressure of competitive commerce, the preponderating influences of trade and literature, and those social, fiscal, and political forces which are generated by a swift-moving and all-powerful development. It would be the height of folly for Canadians to ignore continental facts and forces, and set themselves against the inevitable, or by wrongful policies seek to interrupt the flow and result of natural sequence. And it is nothing short of crime for our representatives at Washington to

treat the so-called Canadian question as if it were one of present paltry gain of dollars and cents, whose total is too inconsiderable, in the great bulk of national commerce, to be worthy of attention. Ottawa and Washington should act with large intelligence, not with petty scrutiny of petty things, and with one great thought ever in mind, that this vast continent and all the people on it are, by wise management, to be welded into one mighty and homogeneous nation, and that, too, speedily. To me there are no Canadians as distinct from us in the States. I refuse to regard them in that light. We are, upon this continent, already seventy millions of Celtic, Saxon, and German blood — the three bloods that rule the world to-day, and are to rule it for all the future — and we are all Americans, no more separate than Georgia is separate from Vermont or New York from Ontario. And, hence, I say, I am glad that Fort Montgomery was never completed, and trust it never will be. Its casemates and its cannon represent the past, a past forever dead and buried, and not the present, much less the future. There has been enough of war and blood upon the Riche-

lieu. Let there be no more forever. For centuries it was the Rivière aux Iroquois, and
savages made it a river of blood. Then came
the white man, and for two hundred years it
was the river Richelieu, and the refined barbar-
ism of cultured courts, plotting cabinets, and
ambitious ministers crimsoned its current, its
sedges and its lilies, with the blood of armies.
But we have come to happier times, and to-day
the pleasure yacht, the happy tourist, the heavy
boat of commerce type it, and the merry laugh
and lover's song, in the place of rifle and cannon-
shot, are heard in the bright daylight and the
dewy evening between its maples and its wil-
lows.

Fort Montgomery can but be of great interest to the tourist, and will well repay a visit of
inspection. It was built by day's work, and
under inspection of officers of ability, and at a
cost, even as it stands, of over three millions of
dollars to the government. There is no fortress
in the country that will give a visitor a better
idea of what a first-class military work is than
this structure at the outlet of Lake Champlain.
It is in plain view from the Central Vermont

Railroad, and but a short distance from the track. Yachts and boats can approach it from the water-side to the very walls; it is thus most easy of access to the travelling public, and will prove to those who visit it a most instructive and suggestive spectacle.

THE RIVER RICHELIEU.

The roots of a nation's history are in its rivers. They were its earliest pathways, and its infant trade was nursed upon their banks. On them its pioneer life was lived, its earliest battles fought, and its first sufferings borne. Along their banks its experimental crops were grown, and on the current between them floated to market. The rivers of a land are its most ancient highways, and he who travels observingly on them is brought face to face with the olden times.

The Richelieu — all unknown as it is to the average American — is a marvel among rivers. There is, perhaps, no other river on the globe of equal length that can match it with traditions so potent to quicken the imagination or with a history so closely connected with the progress of the human race. To the red man it was known as the Rivière aux Iroquois, so called from Labrador to Lake Huron, because the savage Iroquois used it as the great highway of their hostile forays into the North. In the skin tent of the Esquimaux, in the bark wigwam of the Montagnais at the mouth of the Saguenay, in the great Indian villages of Lake Huron, and in the buffalo-skin tepee of the Western Indians, this river was called by one and the same name — the name of their dreaded foes, that no distance intimidated and no opposition appalled. There was no river on the continent that had so wide a fame before the white man came as this stream which delivers the waters of Lake Champlain into the St. Lawrence.

Then came the white man. French ambition builded its eyrie on the lofty and bald promontory of Quebec. Dutch commerce centred its growing trade on Manhattan Island, and the Puritans laid the foundations of a commonwealth around Massachusetts Bay. And for two hundred years this water-course became the great highway between the hostile forces thus gathered at the North and the South.

Great armies, year after year, toiled up and floated down its stream. Health and sickness, the wounded and the well, the living and the dying, came and went on its current. Between its verdant banks, first of white men who ever saw them, came Champlain. Then follow Frontenac, Montcalm, Wolfe, Arnold, Montgomery, Schuyler, Sullivan, Carlton, Dieskau, Johnson, Putnam, Rogers, and all the great chiefs and scouts of the old wars. All these with their thousands and tens of thousands of followers, titled and unknown alike, came and went with the years along this stream. The great Richelieu and the greater Pitt, kings, generals of fame and noted diplomats, have all studied intently the rude maps on which this little waterway was traced, as men study the cause and course of war, and the way to victory and empire. There is Bloody Isle, whose sands and sedgy reeds have many a time been red with human blood. There is Isle le Noix, with its old earthworks, within whose embankments an army might fight, and where many an army has stood. The elms now grow full seventy feet in height upon their grassy curvature, and in the long summer days white lambs nibble and play in the old embrasures where cannon once exploded. There is the Cove of Death, where bloodiest ambush once was made, and where red and white men fought with knife and tomahawk, and rifle-clubbed, until the shallow channel was paved with bodies, so thick and deep that the living made of them a causeway over which they plunged to get at each other's throats. There is scarcely a curve in this stream, or point reaching out into it, or isle or sandbar, that has not been fought over time and time again by men who fought each other face to face and breast to breast. I doubt if any stretch of river of equal length in any country on the globe has so much of history in it as this little waterway only some seventy miles in length, known as the Richelieu.

And yet, how little is this fact appreciated even by the intelligent portion of the great Republic whose liberty and prosperity, ay, even whose existence as an historic possibility, more than once depended on the fate of martial expeditions that came and went along its tide!

Moreover, it is a most lovely river; lovely to

see and to sail on. Next to the Racquette, as it
was before man destroyed its beauty, I remember it as as lovely a bit of water as I ever
boated.   It is a stream of gentle current, green
flowery banks with many a curve and charming
stretch, well canopied with maples, and fringed
with shrubberies that scent the air with their
sweet odors.   It is an easy day's paddle or sail
from the lake to St. John.   In a steam-launch
it could be made, both the coming and the going, the excursion of a day.   To all who read
this book, I commend it as one that cannot fail
to prove most enjoyable in the act, and delightful in reminiscence.   It is an actual loss to one
who loves the beautiful or appreciates the historic, not to have traversed this section of the
Richelieu.

PART II.

THE GREAT NATIONAL PARK.

If the reader will take a map of the country, and, beginning at Niagara Falls, draw a line eastward to Mount Desert, and, with this as the central line, construct a parallelogram, he will have embraced within it such a grouping of natural scenery both as regards sublimity and beauty, along with such a multitude of resources for human recreation and entertainment, as may not be found elsewhere in connection, either on this continent or in Europe. In Niagara he beholds a world-renowned marvel. To it there is, among waterfalls, no rival on the globe. It is a majestic appearance of nature. In its awful exhibition, majesty and sublimity reveal their highest expression. In its contemplation the beholder enjoys an experience which can never be repeated. He sees, he feels, and out of that

seeing and feeling there grows up and with
him remains forever a magnificent memory.
Niagara is at once the sublimest of spectacles
and the most impressive of recollections.

Northward of the great cataract flows the
St. Lawrence; a river which surpasses all others
in the world in the mystery of its origin,[1] the
length and number of its tributaries, the enor-
mous amount of water it delivers to the ocean,
the evenness of its flow,[2] the multitude of its
rapids and islands'; the varied loveliness of its
riparian scenery, and the dim traditions and historic memories which haunt, like summer reflec-
tions of night and day, its glassy stream.

Thirty years ago the Thousand Islands were
scarcely known to the American public. To-day
they are noted from one end of the country to

---

[1] The Five Great Lakes which make the St. Lawrence a geographical wonder are themselves a mystery. Geology cannot
explain them. Even that stupendous Guess known as the Glacial
Theory loses its audacity in the presence of these phenomena.
Even its imagination, which soars like the frigate bird above
human knowledge and never touches earth, tumbles ignomini-
ously to the ground as it comes to these inland oceans, and con-
fesses it is unable to suggest the cause of these stupendous excava-
tions at the level centre of the continent.

[2] It is said that the St. Lawrence does not change its level eight
inches the whole year round.

the other. The charm of their tranquil loveliness is as delightful to the mind as the spectacle of Niagara is appalling. ' The poet and
scholar, the artist and philosopher, the weary
business man and college student, the angler and
tourist, — that hiveless bee that buzzes from
flower to flower and gathers sweetness only for his
own transient entertainment, — wealth, fashion,
and fame, all resort to this picturesque section
of the noble river, as fairies of every order are
said in elfin lore to gather once each year at the
most lovely centre of fairyland. If our Eastern
country had no other attractions for the tourist
and lover of nature than Niagara and the
Thousand Islands, these alone would make it
famous, and draw from the South and West
thousands upon thousands of visitors each year.

But what may we say of the Adirondacks.
that Venice of the woods, whose highways are
rivers, whose paths are streams, and whose carriages are boats? Thirty years ago they were a
wilderness, a wild, unvalued section of the
Empire State, unknown and unnoted save to
a few sportsmen and their guides. Suddenly
they were revealed. A little volume was pub-

lished which told of their extent, their charming characteristics, their sanitarian qualities, and
their provisions for sport. The great, ignorant,
stay-at-home, egotistic world laughed and jeered
and tried to roar the book down. They called
it a fraud and a hoax. The pictorials of the
day blazoned their broadsides with caricatures of
"Murray and his fools." Innumerable articles
were written to the press, and editorials published, denying that there was any such extent
of woods in the State, any such number of lakes,
any such phenomenal connection of waterways,
any such possibilities of pleasure and health as
the little book portrayed. It should be remembered that there were then no hotels in the
woods, no railroad facilities of entrance and
exit, no accommodation for sick or well, no
moneyed interest, as there is to-day, to assist the
influence of that first publication. But the
facts of geography and the truth of nature were
in it, and it successfully breasted the current
of adverse criticism and hostile comment, of
innuendo and jeer, and carried the fame of the
woods over the continent; and to-day there is
no spot betwixt the two oceans or the two

gulfs better known or more loved by those who
visit them than the far-famed Adirondacks.

Many years have passed since I visited them.
And since I kindled my last campfire on the
Racquette I have lighted many in many places,
and as widely apart as the continent would
allow. And I can well imagine that many
changes have come to the woods whose quietude
and loneliness and the absence of the coming
and going of men made them so attractive to
me when, in other years, I visited them. They
even say that the little wild island I loved in
the Racquette, and on whose ledge of rock,
under untouched trees, I built my lodge, has
been civilized by the axe and the plough, and
that the divine silence of the Sabbath air is
jarred into discord by the clang and rattle of a
chapel bell! But, in spite of all these sad
changes and profanations, I doubt not that the
woods still have their beauty, the mountains
keep their majesties, the lakes glass storm and
shine by day and the stars at night, and that
the pools are as clear and cool as of yore, albeit
they lack the flash and gleam of finny splendor
which shot them through and through with color

in the days when I checked their smooth surface
with my trailing flies.

Yes, the woods are still there, the mountains
abide, the lakes murmur converse to the shores,
the rivers flow on, the pools still go round, and
the trees in the warm nights drop their odorous
gums to the scented mould, as they did when I
saw and heard and breathed their beauty and
perfume. And while these remain, the Adirondack wilderness must ever be what it is to-day,
the most unique, picturesque, charming, and
healthful section of the continent ; the one place
for all to visit, and which not to have seen is to
remain untravelled.

But what shall we say of the Horicon,[1] of
Au Sable Chasm, of the springs of Saratoga, of
the valley of the Le Moile, of the Green Mountains, whose ridges should be white with hotels,
of the Upper Connecticut and Winnipiseogee, of
the White Mountains, of which no one has

---

[1] I do not insist on this name, but I do insist that the name of
the coarse, stupid Hanoverian King of England shall not be used
to designate this most wild and impressive of American lakes. *Lac
St. Sacrement* is not appropriate, Lake George is a vulgarization,
and, if it cannot be known as *Lac aux Iroquois* — Lake of the Iroquois — which is doubtless its truest name, then I prefer the name
that Cooper used to designate it, — the Horicon — Silvery Water.

written fittingly since that priest of God and of
nature both, Starr King, died? For the eye that
sees not only the outward form but the inner
spirit which the form conceals from most; the
ear that hears not only the undulating sound
which strikes all ears alike, but the voice which
dwells within the sound and is alone worth hearing because it alone signalizes it with meaning;
the nose which distinguishes between the
breaths it draws, divides common from uncom-
mon air, and calls that only worthy of praise
that is distinguished with some fine quality; a
choice perfume, a rare fragrance, a pungent
trace of ozone, — that unembodied vitalness
breathed into lower atmospheres out of God's;
he who has not these and other rare gifts is not
fitted to write of woods and waters, of lakes and
mountains, of day and night, as they come from
and go into eternity, because he cannot sense
their high significance or materialize their fine
volatile qualities into the solid, opaque characters of human language. These gifts King had,
and, had he lived, he would have interpreted
the White Hills as they deserve. But, alas, he
died, killed, as was the poet White, by the

fervid zeal of his own genius; and the famous
mountains remain without a prophet until this
day.

Within this parallelogram, moreover, are the
Rangeley Lakes, and Moosehead; Bar Harbor
and Mount Desert, and Poland Springs; and
nigh to its southern line are the beaches of New
Hampshire and Massachusetts, Lexington and
Bunker Hill. And fringing the eastern end of
it are the caribou and moose regions of
northern Maine and New Brunswick, the
salmon rivers that are to anglers as the magnet
is to grains of steel, and but a little way
beyond lie the peaceful meadows of Acadia,
and the home of Evangeline.

Now at the centre of this marvellous parallelogram, crowded as it is with wonders of
nature, with every class of scenery known to
mountains and forests, rivers and lakes, and
provided with every provision for sport and
recreation, pleasure and health, which the enterprise and money of men can provide, is located
Lake Champlain, in many respects the most
interesting and attractive section of the whole.
It is characterized by the length and breadth of

its waters; the multitude and loveliness of its islands; the majesty of its surrounding mountains; the pastoral beauty of its shores, and the historic memories with which it is and must ever remain in vital and vivid connection.

For the lover of aboriginal traditions and relics it supplies a field absolutely unexplored. To the angler it gives a habitat of the black bass as abundantly stocked as any other stretch of American water. To the yachtsman it affords opportunities of pleasure, navigation, and amateur seamanship as ample as sound or ocean coast supply, while to the canoeist and campist it extends, in its bays and rivers, its islands and its shores, its golden beaches and bold promontories, ideal conditions of recreation and enjoyment, and the health which comes to those who love the outdoor life and world.

Nor is it less remarkable for its connections. The Adirondacks come to its western beach, and the Green Mountains slope gradually down to its eastern shore. The Chasm of the Au Sable is within easy walk of it, and the Horicon is its nigh neighbor. The ruins of Ticonderoga and Crown Point are on it, and the delights of the

Hudson within a few hours' travel, while by its outlet to the north the steam-launch and sailing-yacht can glide downward to the broad St. Lawrence, and thence go upward to the Thousand Islands or downward to Quebec, Montmorency, and the Saguenay. Its waters are traversed by steamers that, in size and appointments, are excelled only by the floating palaces of Long Island Sound, and the railways that touch it at many points enable the tourist to pass, by day or night, in any direction. Intelligently estimated, and weighed in the balance of considerate comparison, it is the most beautiful lake on the continent, and to him who sees it ·for the first time it is both a revelation and an education.

Congress may resolve and newspaper correspondents may with hasty pen declare that this or that spot, distinguished by some local phenomena, shall be known as the National Park, but neither formal resolution nor hasty verdict of casual writers can change the geography of the continent or the facts of nature; and these declare — and with an emphasis that cannot be misunderstood or unheeded by the intelligent — that the *Great National Park, for the whole American people*, lies within the lines of the parallelogram I have suggested, and to it there is not now, and never can be, on the continent, a rival. Niagara, the Thousand Islands, the Adirondacks, the Horicon, Champlain with its battle memories, the White Mountains, and the coast of Maine are all in it, and there they will remain forever. These great and admirable objects of nature can never be removed either to the south or west, but will abide where God has placed them; and to them, to see, to admire, to marvel, and enjoy, will the thousands and millions of the American people who love nature and have reverence for shrines annually journey.

It was on the shores of the Atlantic that the Republic was born. Here was she cradled, and here was her early loveliness grown. The American people know this fact, and to the East will the millions continue to come as to the birthplace of the nation. The continental lines of travel will cross the continent from ocean to ocean, not from gulf to gulf, and the millions upon millions that are in the years to come to people the prairies and valleys of the Great West will seek recreation and pleasure among the hills and lakes, the rivers and mountains, of the section I have suggested, and which is, by nature and fact, and is destined to be called, *The Great National Park of the Republic.*

If those who now control the present lines of travel, and who, with their successors, should naturally construct the additional accommodations as called for, are wise, they will do well to bear in mind that the places the people want to see are here in the East, and that the great bulk of the people who would fain see them are in the West. The places are here, the people are there, and how to bring people and places together easily and quickly is the problem for them to solve. The pleasure resorts of which we have spoken find their patrons to-day chiefly from the cities of the Atlantic Coast. But the population east of the Alleghanies and the Great Lakes is but a small fraction of the mighty total which represents the nation. The sceptre of numbers has already passed to the prairies, and the sceptre of wealth is sure to follow. But what are these compared with those great centres of population which will be grouped here and there clean across the great basin which extends westward to the Rocky Mountains? It is not beyond reason to believe that at least one of those Western cities will have, within fifty years, more inhabitants than Philadelphia, New York, and Boston combined. If the causes which have given London its five millions are not so exceptional as never to be operant again or elsewhere, then is it as certain as the sun shines that Chicago, at some period not remote, will have within her corporate limits from ten to fifteen millions of people.

If the Republic endures in peace and prosperity, there surely will be gathered within two centuries on the shore of Lake Michigan a city which for the wealth and number of its citizens, the magnificence of its appearance, and the power of the forces it represents, has never been equalled since men were grouped into nations, felt the force of centralization, and built cities to express the grandeur of their ambitions and the glory of their civilization.

The old New-England nests are empty and
cold because the young birds which once filled
and warmed them with life have flown abroad.
With their wings came longings, and singly and
in flocks they went forth to find new places for
new nests and new colonies. But the lines of
their flight were not hidden, and the world
knows whither they went and where they are.
But with them went love for the old places and
memory ; and the sons and daughters of New
England remember her mountains and her
lakes, her rivers and her shores, and the homes
of their fathers. Nor will they ever forget her
hilltops and her valleys. These and their descendants still see the stars of the East and
love them, and while blood is thicker than
water and prosperity abides with the nation, a
long and ever growing procession of men and
women, half pilgrims and half tourists, will
with the coming of summer and autumn journey eastward to see the fields and woods, the
lakes and hills that their forefathers saw, and
rekindle the torch of family affection at the
hearthstones of their ancestors. The West and
the East of the nation stand connected as

children are connected with parents and midday is related to morning.

I foresee the day, not as remote but nigh, when the Great Lakes shall be utilized for the purposes of pleasure as fully as for traffic; when magnificent steamers shall take the summer tourists at Chicago wharves and transport them eastward; when the Thousand Islands and Niagara shall be in direct water connection for excursionists from the West; when long trains of palace cars shall run direct, without change, from Chicago, St. Louis, Minneapolis, and Denver to the Adirondacks, Lake Champlain, and the White Mountains; the lovely Winnipesaukee, the lakes of Maine and its celebrated beaches; when the great pleasure resorts of the nation, which are here and ever will remain here in the East, will be in as direct and facile connection with the cities of the West as are Philadelphia, New York, and Boston to-day; and I anticipate that this annual visitation of thousands from the West to the East, as prompted by the love of pleasure, of health and ancestral memories, will not be the least among those unifying forces upon which we must rely to preserve the great Republic, as its millions multiply, in the unity which is born from and maintained by mutual acquaintance and affection between its widely separated sections.

PART III.

LAKE CHAMPLAIN AND THE FACILITIES IT OFFERS TO YACHTSMEN.

EACH summer the tide of travel on the Atlantic slope sets with a stronger and deeper current northward. The mountains and the sea, the woods and the beaches are in rivalry, and slowly but surely the mountains and the woods are winning. The cities of the seaboard are like ovens each summer, and thousands come pouring out of them when driven by the awful heat, crying, " Whither shall we go? "

To the seashore? Certainly, if you cannot find a better resort; but all of us know that the seashore is but little better than the oven, and often worse. The dead glare, hour after hour, on the level and blistering sea; the rank smells of the marsh bogs and the oozy flats steaming stenchfully under the hot rays when the tide is out; the night fogs and chilly, damp

mornings; the soppy mists which roll their
wetness even into your sleeping-chamber; and
then the dismal, rainy mornings when the grass
is as seaweed and all the trees drip cheerlessly,
oh, I know well what the much-lauded seashore
is, for I was born on it.

Lord Byron is the only one who ever made
the sea attractive. He pitched the resonance of
his verse to the keynote of its thunder, and
sent the jar and terror of its waves through the
structure of his stanzas, so that they roll and
reel and come tumbling down upon you as you
read, as billows upon a beach — thunderingly.
He too, gifted being as he was, could catch its
softer moods and make its whispers run along
his lines so coyly and soothingly that the reader
is made, perforce, to admire its majesties and
gentleness. But all the time, if you be a coast-
born man, you have an uneasy feeling that the
poet is fooling you — that it is all false and not
true which you are reading; a poetic fiction and
not the actual fact.

And that is the case truly. For the sea is
murderous, cruel, and catlike in its treacherous
habits, and all shore men know it. It tempts

one out upon its surface, toys with you for an hour most pleasantly to yourself; then suddenly and fiercely tosses you up, and you, coming down beneath an overturned boat, — why, the "beautiful sea" has enriched its vast death-chamber with another corpse!

Two yachtsmen, after storm, — out of whose clutch their yacht had been wrenched as by the hand of God, — were strolling on a beach one morning, with the dear old pines on the one hand and the dread billows still rolling hungrily on the other, when, clambering around a point of slippery rocks, they suddenly saw, half embedded in the sand, two white faces lying side by side. A man's and woman's face, both young, lying so closely that the pale cheeks almost touched. Doubtless they had, when warm with life, touched each other lovingly a thousand times, for surely these two lying thus on a foreign beach, a thousand leagues from home, were lovers, death-mated. They were young emigrants seeking by faith another and a better country. God grant they found it!

See his strong boots reaching heavily above

the knee, and her stout shoes. But how shapely
the full foot within, and how finely death has
marbled it in beauty! Poor, brave little foot,
thou didst come to the end of thy journey suddenly. Thy sunrise was thy noonday and
thine evening too! See the sand in the man's
beard. The sand is so like the hair in color
that thou must look close to see the sifted
grains. And the young woman's, what a sable
wealth was given her for ornament! How
could hers be so black, she being a German
girl? Or was there in her veins a dash of that
old race, older than Egypt's, who for unnumbered ages dwelt where Spain now is; who,
tradition says, conquered the world, and the
swarth beauty of whose women can be found
here and there to-day on every shore of the
round earth? I know not. I only know that
two yachtsmen found one morning two faces
lying half embedded in the sand; one of a
man, the other a woman's; the man's beautifully blond, the woman's gloriously dark;
lying so closely each to the other that they
almost touched, and so saying, "Oh, finder of
us, we are two lovers murdered by the dreadful

sea; but we kissed each other in the white surf out yonder before we died."

But what shall I say of the unseen faces — the faces that disappear in storm and wreck and are never found? Have I not time and again sat on the gray rocks by the sea line with closed eyes and seen them stretch away in rows, a hundred, a thousand white faces, all having the same white, rigid look on them? Yes, I have seen the bottom of the sea revealed — a hell of sight — the still white faces, and above and among them the dreadful creatures that eat them — the creatures that make the life of the sea; the eyeless and sightless things that are directed in their courses by other senses than that of sight. You love the sea? Love it then in your ignorance, and thank God you are ignorant, or else can see nothing save the surface. A great and dreadful deceit is the sea, and we who have sailed on it know it.

But the woods, the dear, frank, innocent woods. God bless them! They kill no one. At their sweet roots no lovers, sleeping, die. Along their green edges no man and maiden lie side by side, dead, killed by their treachery.

Once in a hundred years, perhaps, one man, and he by accident, is killed by the falling of a tree — some poor, dead tree that could not stand one instant longer, nor help from falling just then and there. Ay, the dear woods that kill no one, tempt no one, but rather warn you to keep out of their depths, near their bright margins, where the sun shines, flowers bloom, and open spaces are; the woods that cool you so with their stored coolness; rest you so with their untaxed restfulness; that never moan of nights because they have killed any one, but rather because any one, for any cause, must be killed, the world over. Yes, yes. John was right. There will be "no sea there!" Had he been shipwrecked? Had he some morning strolling on the beaches of the Isle of Patmos found two white faces embedded in the sand? No matter from what cause or by what awful fact inspired with shrinking, the old Divine Dreamer sensed the truth. Man has wreck and death enough here. It is only just that he should journey beyond it when he enters the vast hereafter.

I predict, therefore, that the great tide of

American travel will soon set northward away from the treacherous, murderous, dirty sea, to the frank, clean woods that are inland, and which make all this far north country sweet with their odorous gums, even to the white line where snow never melts. Oh, if I might only spend my years beneath the trees, eat under them, sleep under them, work, dream, and die under them! How strange that when Heaven waits only on the decision of our wills we refuse to say the word or take the step, and so adjourn it indefinitely until by the passage of that swift force which we name death we are pushed suddenly out of our hesitation and are in our heaven, perhaps "in the twinkling of an eye."

What companionship there is in trees! Who ever saw two alike? This one — a mighty trunk — is vast and round, and smooth as an Egyptian column. Yonder there stands a group, seven in all, grave as statesmen, —

"On whose ivied brows the cares of nations sit."

The central one suggests the Websterian type, strong, rough, and massive. Others yonder are sprightly, suave, and pliant, polite, insinuating;

while others, on that island there, are simply
gigantic posts with sap in them, that stand like
the old Dutch burghers in heaviest armor, perfectly symbolizing the old Dutch motto, " Made
to stand, not run." Not a bad motto, friend,
by which to shape the character of your boy in
these fickle times of ours. And then, how
chatty trees can be. Naturalists tell us that in
all forms of life there is sex. The trees are,
therefore, male and female, and have their court-
ships and their wooings too. Perhaps there are
flirtations among them; who can tell? If so,
how delicious they must be, for their concealment is so perfect!

I take it that, all things considered, yachting
is the most healthful and manly recreation a
man can take, and that, in all the conditions of
enjoyment to the average lover of nature, yachting in inland waters is superior to yachting on
the outer seas. For inland boating, while the
yachtsman, beyond doubt, misses the impressive
grandeur of the outer sea. its magnificent exhi-
bitions of force and the grave majesty of its
vast spaces, he is, on the . other hand, the
recipient of many favors which appeal delight-

fully to his senses and minister in a rare degree to his mind and soul.

To an American yachtsman, especially, inland yachting has a peculiar charm, and yields him a singular enjoyment. His is the only country inhabited by civilized nations which, in its size and facilities of water communication, is continental. To say that a yacht of eight or ten tons can be sailed by a party of tourists four or five thousand miles without passing out of inland waters, and never over the same course twice, is a statement calculated to astound a European, and even an American, we fancy, would have to look up his geography a little to credit it. But. if he will take his map, he will see at a glance how easily the thing can be done, and that the five thousand miles can easily be made ten thousand, if the party can extend its vacation time a month or so. Burlington, or rather this lake lying in front of Burlington, is the natural centre and starting-point for such magnificent touring. It is large enough to supply facilities for aquatic training requisite for such as, not having it, must prepare themselves for these splendid voyages. It is the only lake in all this east country of ours that can serve as a school in which practical knowledge of yachts and yachting can be taught. It is, moreover, so placed as to be easily accessible from the great seaboard cities, from which the majority of our true tourists and sportsmen come. It is surrounded by natural scenery of the highest order. Its shores and bays are alive with historic memories, which quicken patriotism and ennoble the character of whosoe'er receives their inspiration. Here are ruins of ancient forts. Here the lines of old-time earthworks still stand. Here nature has accumulated chasm, gorge, and mountains for the lover of the grand and picturesque to admire, and he who sails its blue water recalls that in days that are past the two most martial races of all the world, and the two rival civilizations of modern times, stood for a hundred years in arms, and contended fiercely for no less a prize than the possession of the American continent. Verily, what other lake can offer the young yachtsman the opportunity to learn the art of sailing his little craft safely amid such enjoyable and inspiriting surroundings as can this one, located as it is nigh the great centres of our population, and amid the noblest sights of nature?

Observe, moreover, the water connections of this lovely and extended lake. Sailing hence, the yachtsman finds an easy outlet through the Richelieu River to the St. Lawrence — that marvellous stream along whose level channel half the fresh water of the globe, it is said, is poured downward to the sea. The Richelieu River takes him to the St. Lawrence; down its broad current he descends to Quebec, whose prominence in American history lifts it more loftily before the student's mind than the rocky promontory on which it stands lifts it before his eyes. Downward still he floats until he beholds Montmorenci's fleecy falls, whose waters leap from a loftier height than Niagara plunges. Below he finds the shrine of St. Anne, around which pilgrims by the thousand kneel each year, and realize the miraculous powers of heaven, as the suppliants are said to have realized it of old. Still downward he sails past the Isle of Bacchus, as Jacques Cartier called the beautiful island we have foolishly dubbed the Isle of Orleans; past the huge bulk of Tourmente,

until we come abreast of the stupendous exhibition of nature called the entrance to the
Saguenay, and creep inward through the gloomy
portal to such a vision as mortal man never
shuddered at elsewhere. And what shall we
say of the sail up this strange and solemn
waterway, which the old mariners verily believed, and plainly stated, led to hell — or of
Tadousac, that oldest town site, perhaps, on the
continent; or of the Rivière du Loup, where, in
the warm lush summer days, the government
of Canada and gathered aristocracy hold high
carnival, and politicians play lawn tennis and
croquet, while playing far deeper games and
for nobler prizes than these light ones can yield?
Or of Dalhousie, far, far below, where the Bay
of Chaleur invites and warns the yachtsman,
and the most stupendous fossil trees on all the
globe lie half embedded in the worn banks for
the tourist to gaze and marvel at? Verily is
not this an excursion the like of which has
never been taken by any party on this continent? And when the little yacht comes sailing
back from this fair cruise, should she not be
cheered right roundly for the demonstration she

has made; a demonstration in the interest of
outdoor life and sport, and of all who love the
airs of health, the sights and sounds of nature,
and would fain encourage and advance the
innocent pleasures of the world and help set
the fashion, which, if followed for a few genera-
tions by the people, will fill the land with fair
women and manly men?

Or if the party be of those who love the
"gentle art," what a voyage it would be! For
is there better ground for rod and reel than
Champlain and the tributaries of the St. Lawrence afford? Black bass — what true angler
does not love the sturdy fish that "fights it
out" to the bitter end, and yields the battle
only with his life? And are there nineteen
miles of coast, from Quebec downward to the
mouth of the Restigouche and the Miramichi,
that he does not sail past the mouth of streams
that are the haunt of salmon and sea trout,
while every tumbling torrent on either shore is
full of spotted trout, that jump for joy to see
the "fair deceit" trail past their cool retreats?
Verily the true angler should love the little
yacht that can thus waft him to such sport, and

bring him cheerily home with flowing sails from
scenes and victories which will keep the torch
of memory aglow, and brighten with its gentle
ray the darkness of descending years. Or if
he loves the rifle, and is not timid of the autumn
gale, can he land on either shore for a hundred
leagues and not be in the very home of the
moose and the caribou, and on waters speckled
with ducks and geese and brant? Or, if he
loves the silent forests, the blazed line, and the
untrodden mosses of deep woods, can he not
push his solitary trail northward to the Lake
St. John, and farther yet — if he be ambitious
and fearless — to that recently rediscovered
lake known to the Jesuits, but lost to human
knowledge for two hundred years, the mysteri-
ous Mistassinni? Surely here, in this vast
region, stretching clean from the northern bank
of the St. Lawrence to Hudson Bay, the born
woodsman can find the loneliness he loves, and
the furred animals in whose capture he finds
full exercise of his skill and the vigorous
pleasure of watchful, busy days and weird
nights. And all these pleasures, and many
beside, can be had by him who owns, and sails

knowingly, his little yacht with a month's
leisure at his command, from the blue waters of
Burlington Bay.

But one does not need to sail beyond the
waters of Lake Champlain itself to find enjoyment to satisfy the most exacting. For here
one can find, in the highest degree, experiences
to satisfy both soul and sense. The lake is large
enough to accommodate the yachtsman with
a month's cruising, during which no day shall
be a repetition of the preceding ones. Of all the
lakes in our great country, Champlain is, by
common consent of those acquainted with its
characteristics, the most beautiful. The Horicon
is certainly the most charming and picturesque,
but it lacks breadth of view, and affords the eye
no grandeur of perspective. It is pent, confined, and too closely fenced by the hills and
mountains which rise from its very shore line, to
allow the eye to gaze widely and far off. I
have camped and boated on it much and often,
and am free to confess that after a few weeks
I always wearied of it, and longed for a wider
stretch of water and those perspectives of
vision which, because of their dim distance,

perhaps, and the changes in line and color, never
tire or appear the same, as the days multiply.
Memphremagog and Winnipesaukee are most
lovely bits of inland water, but they also are
too small and otherwise unfitted for yachting.
You can picnic, but you cannot journey on them,
and a perpetual picnic is as tiresome as a perpetual camp-meeting.　But Lake Champlain has
width and length, broad spaces and extensive
views.　You can sail one hundred and thirty
miles in a straight line from north to south; its
bays are many and deep, and each has its characteristics which distinguish it from the others,
and make for the artistic eye a separate study,
and give to the lover of the beautiful in nature
a fresh and pleasurable sensation.　Then, too,
from what other lake in all the land can one
behold such mountain scenery as from Champlain?　To the west for one hundred miles, loom
the Adirondacks, with their myriad peaks cloud-
capped or clearly outlined against the farther
sky.　To the east the Green Mountains, far
enough away to show at their best, lift their
lofty sides, verdant to their summits; while in
the lake itself float islands of all shapes and

sizes, from the pillar of brown rock tufted with its dwarf pines, to Grand Isle, to circle which you must fetch a circuit of fifty miles. Champlain is no pond, no narrow, petty lake even, but a great body of long, wide water, where winds can blow and blue waves roll as on some deep, broad arm of the sea itself. Moreover, Lake Champlain is historic to a degree beyond any other body of water in America. At Tadousac, at the mouth of the Saguenay, and at Quebec, the student senses the antique as the nose inhales the aroma of flowers blown through the air by noiseless winds from afar. But before Quebec was founded, Champlain's arquebus, right opposite Burlington here, had shed Iroquois blood, and started a terrible echo among the hills above Crown Point, which died not away until it was finally drowned by the crash of Wolfe's musketry on the Plains of Abraham, one hundred and fifty years later. From the northern end of this famous lake, up the Richelieu came Frontenac, came Montcalm, came Burgoyne, came all those great martial movements, whether under French or English banners, which, during the early or later wars, threatened the whole south country, which flowed victoriously on, and were not stopped until the Hudson itself was sighted from the ruins of Fort William Henry and the heights above Saratoga. Along these shores on the west, Putnam and Rogers scouted and fought. Here is Plattsburg Bay and Cumberland Head, where Macdonough fought his glorious fight. Here, off Vergennes, chased by the English admiral, Arnold fired his ship, whose timbers can be seen through the clear waters to-day. Here is Ticonderoga, in front of whose fatal abattis Abercrombie left two thousand of his bravest dead, and within whose walls Ethan Allen demanded its surrender "in the name of God and the Continental Congress." But why enumerate? There is scarcely a bay or promontory upon the lake that has not some historic recollections clustering around it, half of them unwritten. For here History sits holding her unlettered scroll, waiting for some Prescott or Parkman to write upon them the marvellous stories of other and heroic days, when English civilization and American liberty successively contended for victory upon the bosom and along the sides of this lake.

I foresee the day when a thousand pleasure yachts shall whiten these blue waters with their sails, and other thousands of summer cottages shall stretch their line of healthy, happy life along the shores and speck with color the islands of this lake. Why should it not be so? Why should not the seaboard cities turn their eyes this way for summer homes and summer pleasure? Here land is cheap. Here are all the conditions for health. Here is splendid sporting. Here are the rarest facilities for yachting. Here is scenery unsurpassed in the world. Here are excellent food markets easily accessible. Here the telephone and telegraph can connect every cottager with his city business and friends. And here are swift connections by rail not only with the seaboard cities of the States, but with all that is attractive in Canadian scenery and life, from the Bay of Chaleur to Niagara. He who thinks that Lake Champlain and its sightly shores are not destined to be speedily possessed by lovers of the beautiful and seekers of needed rest and health thinks meanly of the average intelligence of the health-seeking, pleasure-loving

American. Fifteen years ago, and the Adirondack region was almost unknown. A few dozens of sportsmen visited it each summer. Twenty houses, mostly built of logs, were all that were there. To-day a hundred thousand people visit the woods each year, and great hotels stand on the shores of little lakes, where then a man might camp in solitude. What has caused this wondrous change? Why do the people by thousands rush thitherward to-day? Simply because the people were told of the sport, pleasure, and health they could find in that then far-off and unknown place. The demand existed. It was met with a supply; knowledge was furnished them, and the people responded promptly, as they always will. That is all that need be said to cover the whole ground.

There are thousands all over the country who know I will not write one word in favor of any sport or place in reference to the benefits to be derived from it by them, if I am not intelligent and well-informed. They know that I do not sell my pen as a hireling to praise what is not praiseworthy. I love the outdoor life and world, the pure air of water stretch, and the

mountain tops, and the pure thought and life
that come to those who breathe it, and I would
that all those who love these things with me
may enjoy them with me. Hence, at times, I
write to them — known and unknown to me by
name and face — to tell them what I have found
and where I have found it — health, peace, and
the new vigor which comes from restful days
and quiet nights, filled through all their dewy
hours with sweet sleep — "sleep which knits
up the ravelled sleave of care," and pleasures
which stimulate the frame and warm the
blood like ancient wine. And to all such I say,
Come to Lake Champlain and spend the summer here. You who love the water, send up your
boats and yachts or build them here, and I will
warrant you such pleasant and spirited yachting as is rarely found. You who love the tent
and social camp-fire, verily is there not room
here for an army of tents, and yet not one
shall see the other; you who need the rest and
health found in pure, cool mountain air, come
to the base of these hills, amid whose tops God
generates the ozone of life, and, floating on the
level water, breathe its vigor in.

The extraordinary facilities which Lake
Champlain offers the yachtsman in his enjoyment of his favorite pastime are not unknown
or unappreciated by many; but to thousands
they are unknown, and hence this publishment.

It is beyond question the safest sailing and
cruising ground that the amateur yachtsman
can find. Here he can serve his apprenticeship
to skill under the best possible conditions.
First and foremost, it is a tideless water. The
given sailing depth on reef and shoal, in channel and mouth of rivers, is a constant one.
Where the yachtsman can go in the morning
he can go at midday and in the moon-lighted
evening; in calm or stormy weather. Those
who, as amateurs and strangers, have sailed the
Atlantic coast or the lower St. Lawrence, with
its ebb and flood of from ten to fifteen feet,
know how to appreciate this fact in its relation
to safety and absence of anxiety on the part of
a skipper. Furthermore Lake Champlain is
long and wide enough for cruising and racing
both. Its bays are deep and its islands many.
Squalls are infrequent and cannot approach the
lake without making plain revelation of their

approach. In case of need, refuge is easily and quickly found behind island or within bay. A fool, it is said, can capsize a boat even behind a breakwater or within a basin, but he who allows any serious accident to befall his yacht on Champlain must be a genius of idiocy. There has never been an accident to a yacht handled by a yachtsman on the lake within my knowledge, and I never expect there will be.

The yachting interest of the lake finds its natural centre at Burlington. In front of this city the lake is wide and free of all obstructions. Here a triangular race of thirty miles can be sailed with every yacht, from start to finish, under the gazer's eye — a very rare condition in regattas. Indeed, we know no other course in front of a city of which this statement can be made. On a pier at the foot of the principal street of the city, within a few rods of the Central Vermont Depot and the wharf of the Champlain Transportation Company, the Lake Champlain Yacht Club has erected its large and commodious clubhouse. No other clubhouse on the continent gives to its members and their guests such a magnificent

vision of natural loveliness and sublimity.
The lake rolls its waves to its doors, and the
motion of its water gives animation to the
scene. From its wide, high balconies the eye
beholds a spectacle of unrivalled loveliness and
majesty. Directly in front and stretching far
to right and left the lake itself, with glint of
sun by day and gleam of stars by night, unrolls
its crystal spaces. To the left, in plain view,
stands Mohawk Rock, dumb reminder of a departed race and immemorial years. To the
right is Bluff Point, to which geologists go to
translate the messages of eternity to time. In
the middle of the lake the islands of the Four
Winds ride at anchor. The nighest point of
the farther shore is that one on which Champlain shot the captive Iroquois chief to save
him from further torture by his Algonquin con-
querors. To the northward, in clear view, Point
Trembleau thrusts its rocky promontory out into
the murmuring water, and with its beach of
iron sand gives to the lake the greeting of the
mountains. While in the west the Adirondack
peaks — a hundred summits crowding upward
in confusion — penetrate the clear atmosphere

and serrate the blue of the farther sky with the edges of their dark formation. To one who admires the beautiful in nature it is worth the ride of a thousand miles to enjoy for a single day and evening the freedom of the balconies and the observation roof of the clubhouse of the Lake Champlain Yacht Club at Burlington.

The club was founded in 1887, and for other uses than mere aquatic sports demand. It was felt by its founders that Lake Champlain would soon attract national attention. The martial splendor of its history and the momentous political significance of the glorious drama, the various and exciting scenes of which had all been played upon its waters and its shores, would compel the interest and presence of thousands upon thousands. The yachtsman, canoeist, and angler would come as a matter of course; but these would constitute but a fraction of the multitude that would visit this most lovely and historic section of the United States —a section where nature seems to have entered into rivalry with tradition and history to demonstrate which might exert the strongest influence on the intelligent and travelling por-

tion of mankind. As well might Lexington,
Bunker Hill, and Plymouth Rock remain un-
visited, as that Isle La Motte, Colchester Point,
Plattsburg, Valcour, Crown Point, Ticonderoga, and Burlington Bay be much longer
neglected by the students of American history
and the tourists of the country. They fully apprehended also the significance of its geographical location — that it lay at the centre, from
east to west, of that remarkable parallelogram
of country which begins with Niagara and the
Thousand Isles and ends at Bar Harbor and
Mount Desert, and within which, beside these
famous localities and resorts of pleasure, are
grouped also the Adirondacks and the Chateau-
gay region, the Horicon and Saratoga Springs,
the Green Mountains and the upper Connecticut, the world-advertised White Hills, the lakes
of Maine, and the justly celebrated fountain of
health at Poland Springs; and connected with
these famous resorts more than five hundred
hotels, to which the visiting guests annually
pay a tribute of more than fifteen millions of
dollars.

The gentlemen who founded the Lake Cham-

plain Yacht Club saw these facts, and that the
lake on which they lived was the natural and
magnificent centre of this marvellous stretch
of country in which Nature, in rivalry with
herself, has crowded every variety of scenery
and every charm that can attract the tourist.
Into this noted parallelogram of space she has
grouped her cataracts and waterfalls; her
gorges and chasms; her mountains and valleys;
her lakes and rivers; stocked these with fish, and
the forest spaces with game; and over all, they
perceived, Tradition had thrown the glamour
of her charm, and that upon the vast and
gloomy front of prehistoric times History had
blazoned the vivid record of glorious transac-
tions. Apprehending these things, they felt that
the God who created this continent and grouped
its marvels in such close connection had, in this
eastern section of it, located the Great National
Park of the Republic and made Lake Champlain
the natural and appropriate centre and central
charm of it.

The club, the originating and establishing
motive of which sprang from such a clear and
noble apprehension, was not created to serve a

local purpose or encourage one fashion of recreation, however manly and desirable; but rather
to disseminate needed and quickening information to the country, and to serve the highest
purposes of patriotism and American social life.
Hence its membership was limited to no class
or locality, nor to national lines; for it was felt
by the originators of the club that the beauty
of the lake was of so high an order, and its
historic associations so influential and far-reaching, as judged in the light of our developing
civilization, that in the truest sense of it, as of
no other body of water on the continent, it
belonged to the entire continent and the whole
world.

Its membership was from the beginning, and
is still, cosmopolitan. It is naturally composed
of gentlemen of intelligence, public spirit and
standing. Many of its members are men of
national fame. Its annual dues are too slight
to be burdensome to any, but ample, from the
largeness of its membership, for all purposes of
needed revenue. As regards yachts and yachting, it has a fleet of nearly forty well-built
boats, which is rapidly increasing. Its sailing

section is composed of catboats, sharpies, Burgess-modelled sloops, and English cutters; nearly all of them new boats and of much larger size than is generally found in amateur clubs. Its clubhouse is not the resort of yachtsmen and canoeists alone, but even in a greater degree of ladies and gentlemen who love the sight of rolling and rippling water; of passing sails and steamers; of green islands and majestic mountains; the shady balcony and cool currents of wind; cheerful companionship and restful quiet. Its rooms and wide verandas are opened and maintained by the members as a favorite noonday and evening resort, a quiet, peaceful lounging-place and restful refuge from office rush and noisy hotel for themselves and their guests. A more delightful one might not be imagined.

Hospitality is the characteristic of American club life, and especially of yachting-club life, and the officers and local members of this club are not behind their brother clubmen in the exercise of this most ancient and honorable of virtues. Not only do all visiting yachtsmen, but all travellers and tourists who visit this remarkable region, receive every possible courtesy at their hands. The club might almost be called a Bureau of Information in the interest of visitors, so willing are its local officers and members to assist the transient guest of the city with all needed knowledge.

I publish in this connection the list of the officers of the club, that all who may wish to correspond with them may know whom to address. It is their desire, as it is of the entire body of the membership of the club, that it should receive additions from every State of the Union and every Province of Canada ; and they do, through my words, make public this desire, and cordially invite all who intend to visit Lake Champlain or would assist them in rendering services to those who do visit it, to unite themselves to the club, that they and their friends may enjoy its privileges and assist them in their efforts to serve the public with courteous assistance and fitting hospitality.

OFFICERS OF THE CLUB.

Commodore, W. Seward Webb; *vice-commodore,* W. A. Crombie ; *president,* J. Gregory Smith ; *first vice-president,* Elias Lyman ; *second vice-president*, H. LeGrand Cannon ; *secretary*, Joseph Auld ; *treasurer*, Horatio Hickok ; *measurer*, A. C. Tuttle ; *fleet captain*, Horatio Loomis ; *fleet surgeon*, A. P. Grinnell, M.D. *Executive Committee:* Horatio Hickok, W. H. H. Murray, A. C. Tuttle, F. W. Smith, D. W. Robinson, C. F. Carter, N. F. Merrill, Elias Lyman, R. G. Severson, Joseph Auld, Alvaro Adsit, J. A. Averill, Jacob G. Sanders, A. C. Whiting, H. M. Phelps, C. A. Murray, F. E. Smith, E. C. Smith, S. W. Cummings, J. G. Hindes, H. H. Noble, Walter C. Witherbee, A. G. Whittemore, W. A. Crombie, Theodore S. Peck, H. J. Brookes, H. LeGrand Cannon, F. J. Hawley, J. B. Tresidder, L. C. Grant, T. P. W. Rogers, Samuel Keyser. *Regatta Committee:* L. C. Grant, Chester Griswold, A. C. Whiting, Horace J. Brookes, M. B. Adams. *House Committee:* H. LeGrand Cannon, W. A. Crombie, T. P. W. Rogers. *Membership Committee:* Horatio Hickok, Elias Lyman, A. C. Whiting, F. W. Smith, W. H. H. Murray. *Committee on Printing:* Horatio Hickok, Joseph Auld, A. G. Whittemore.

SAILING DIRECTIONS.

FROM BURLINGTON GOING NORTH.

Opposite Burlington are no obstructions that are not visible in daylight.

Juniper Island (lighthouse). — To the south is Juniper Reef (buoyed); eight feet on reef at low water; buoy on northwest corner; can go close to it; to the south go one-third of a mile, no nearer to buoy.

Shelburn Bay. — Two miles of safe sailing; free of reefs. North of the mouth of this bay, near the centre of the entrance, a half-mile to the north, is Proctor's Reef; buoy on northwest corner. Can sail near the buoy, but give a quarter of a mile margin if you go to the south of it.

Juniper Island Reef. — Running out toward Mohawk Rock a third of a mile; advise not coasting too near the island unless with pilot.

Four Brothers. —Southwest from Burlington, four miles distance. Give these a quarter of a mile berth to the south, east, and west; to the north three-quarters of a mile, for in that direction there are three reefs, called "Three Bunches" (*not buoyed*). These reefs have at least six feet of water on them. Yachts can land safely on the Brothers in quiet weather. These islands are pleasant ones to visit, and from them a superb view of the lake can be had in all directions.

West by north, almost directly opposite Burlington, is Willsborough Point, and west of the point is the entrance to Willsborough Bay. This bay is about five miles in depth. At the head stands the village of Willsborough. The entrance is free from all obstructions; large yachts can enter and sail the bay to its head safely. This is a beautiful sheet of water, very much land-locked and secluded, so that it in fact seems like a separate lake.

Port Douglas is north of Willsborough Bay some three and a half miles, and has a dock at which yachts could be moored in safety.

Schuyler's Island (Isle Chapon, by the French)

is to the northeast, and water is of good depth
between it and the mainland.

Schuyler's Reef is to the southeast of the
island, some mile and a quarter. It is buoyed
on the east side. In coasting give a third of a
mile to this reef. About six feet of water is
on it, so that to small yachts no danger may be
apprehended in good weather sailing nearer.

Ferris Rock is northeast of Schuyler's Island
about one and a half miles. It is buoyed;
buoy is at the centre. A yacht can sail within
a hundred feet of it safely.

Point Trembleau is a bold, rocky projection
northwest of Schuyler's Island, on mainland,
and has good depth of water in front of it.

Port Kent, one mile to the north, has a good
mooring basin at the dock. The bay between
the dock and Point Trembleau is not good
anchoring-ground; plenty of water, but hard
bottom. Of course, with a northwest or south
wind, yachts would find excellent refuge there,
but should the wind shift to the east or northeast or southeast, anchors would not hold, and
to escape going ashore a yacht would have to
get under way. At Port Douglas, or, better

yet, in Willsborough Bay, in such an event, a yacht could find the best of refuge; or, going behind Valcour Island, in case the wind was from the east or southeast, a yacht would find the safest of accommodation.

North of Port Kent, some two miles, is a bank of sand (buoyed); small yachts can go inside of it, but it is safer to stand outside of it.

Au Sable Point is three miles and more to the north of Port Kent. Southeast of the point, a quarter of a mile from the shore, is a buoy; can sail near it safely, but if the wind is strong from north or east better stand out a little.

Sailing north from Au Sable Point, lay your course centrally between Valcour Island and mainland until you come to the northwest point of the island, when you will find — two-thirds the distance from the island to main shore — a reef (buoyed), with five feet of water on it. Water is of good depth on either side.

Bluff Point is a projection of mainland immediately to the north, and is now made a commanding object by the magnificent hotel recently built upon it.

Crab Island. — Two miles from north end of Valcour Island, due north, is Crab Island. Give this island a berth of nearly a quarter of a mile all round it.

Coming back to Valcour Island, we would say, —

Garden Island is to the south of Valcour a half a mile, and a quarter of a mile east of Garden Island is Garden Island Ledge. This has eight feet of water; safe sailing all round both island and ledge.

On the east side of Valcour Island, about a third of the distance from the southern end, is Smuggler's Cove. This is a small recess of water with a narrow entrance. There is from five to six feet of water in this cove. It is a pretty, secluded spot to lunch or camp in, and a small yacht would find it a very safe and pleasant mooring-ground. There is a little spring of water here, very agreeable, and handy for picknickers.

Sloop Cove is located half-way of the island of Valcour, on the east side. It has only two or three feet of water in it, and hence is not safe to enter unless in case of small, light-draft boats and still weather.

North of Sloop Cove, about a mile distant, is
a rock separated by a short distance from main
shore. We call attention to this rock because
to the north of it, about a quarter of a mile, is
a reef (not buoyed). On it is five and a half
feet of water. This reef is small in extent.
With the exception of this unbuoyed reef, the
entire east side of Valcour Island can be coasted
by yachts of good size safely.

From Valcour Island to Plattsburg is
unobstructed sailing (excepting Crab Island,
previously mentioned). The entrance to Plattsburg Harbor, viz., inside the breakwater, is
plain sailing, and the yachtsman needs no
directions from me.

Cumberland Bay, lying between Plattsburg
and Cumberland Head, is not adapted for
yachts on the western half of it. The eastern
half gives good water. Nevertheless, in case of
a stiff southerly wind I would not advise sailing
in this bay. Better stand out to the south of
Cumberland Head, where the courses are free
of all obstruction.

It is well for skippers of small yachts to
bear in mind that in case of strong southerly

winds the stretch south of Cumberland Head
for ten miles is the roughest on the lake. Such
a wind blows with unobstructed sweep for
nearly thirty miles down the lake. Salt-water
yachtsmen are inclined to underrate the capacity of inland water to test the seagoing ability
of a craft or the skill of a skipper, but we who
sail Champlain — and some of us were born on
the coast and know what "rough water" is —
can testify that a skipper who beats his boat up
the lake from Plattsburg to Burlington with
even half a gale blowing from the south will
have a wet boat and wet sails too before he has
passed Colchester Reef. We, therefore, regard-
ing safety as the first thing to consider in pleasure yachts, advise all small yachts to be careful
of this stretch of water in strong southerly
winds.

Gravelly Point is north of Cumberland Head
some two miles. It is easily recognized by the
gravelly shale that composes the shore. We
call attention to it because from all southerly
and western and northwest wind, it makes a
very fine anchorage ground. The bottom is a
good holding one, and yachts can lie close in

within two hundred feet of the beach in safety.
But in case the wind shifts to the east or north
or northeast, the skipper must move out. In
this case he finds a safe and easy run round
Cumberland Head to Plattsburg.

From Gravelly Point coasting north six miles
brings you to the *Light Tower* (Point au Roche),
and to it is clean sailing with good water. Just
opposite the Light (half a mile) is Point au
Roche Reef, in which is seven feet of water with
good depth on either side.

Isle La Motte is north of Point au Roche
Light some two miles. Take the west side and
you will find good water without obstruction
until you come to the north end of the island,
where you must bear in mind

Point au Fer. — This is one mile to the north
of the Light Tower, on the north end of the
island. It is nearly three-fourths of a mile
long, and should be given a good margin. But
there is nearly a mile width of good sailing
water between it and the island, so no skipper
needs feel troubled.

After passing this reef, the course lies open
to you to *Rouse's Point.* You can sail half a

mile or so from the shore and feel that you have goodly space of good water on either hand. At Rouse's Point is good anchorage and the north-.ernmost one of the lake.

We will now return to Burlington.

Shelburn Bay is about three miles from the clubhouse, and is about two miles deep. It is free of shoals and reefs and is good sailing ground. Good-sized yachts can be sailed to within one-fourth of a mile of its end without danger. If the wind is from the northwest and strong, the water in the bay is quite rough, and in beating back a small sailboat should be carefully handled.

Saxton's Reef is about one and a half miles south of Shelburn Point, and half a mile from shore. It is buoyed on west side. There is eight feet of water on the one part of it and eleven feet on the other. It is safe to go within forty rods on either side of it.

Quaker Smith's Reef is opposite the point of that name and some one and a half miles from Saxton's Reef, bearing south by west from it. It is about three-fourths of a mile from the shore, and has seven feet of water on it. It is buoyed and is of small extent. It is safe to go nigh to it.

Opposite Quaker Smith's Reef is the *Bluff*, and from said bluff there stretches out to the west a shoal for nearly one-fourth of a mile. The point of the shoal has only five and a half feet in it, and should therefore be borne in mind by cruising parties, especially if they are making for

Quaker Smith's Bay. — This bay is back of the point of the same name, and makes excellent anchorage ground for yachts of any size, as it has depth of water from ten to twenty feet and good bottom. It is also perfectly protected from all winds, and has a wide, easy entrance. In entering this bay bear in mind that to the south and east some one-fourth of a mile is a reef with only some five and six feet of water on it.

This bay is the harbor where W. S. Webb, Commodore of the Champlain Yacht Club, moors his several yachts. And during the summer the reef alluded to is buoyed by his care; but the government has no buoy on it.

From Quaker Smith's Point to *Sloop Island,*

opposite Essex, there are no obstructions of any
sort.

About five miles south of Sloop Island some
mile and more you come to *Cedar Beach*, a
favorite resort of campers and picnickers.

Pickett Island, Cedar Island, and *Gardiner
Island*, lie south of Cedar Beach, between it and
Thompson's Point.   East of Gardiner Island,
which is the largest of the three, is good
anchorage for all winds, and there is good depth
of water to get in and out of this fine harbor,
so that no one need fear to push for it if in any
stress.

Thompson's Point is opposite Cloven Rock,
and is a resort of many campers and cottagers.
The waters around it are well stocked with fish,
and anglers find much excellent sport here-
abouts.   Perhaps there is no place on the lake
which is more liked by those who are familiar
with the beauty and sporting facilities of this
locality than Thompson's Point and its adjoin-
ing waters.

Otter Creek is some three miles south of
Thompson's Point.   This creek or river, for in
all rights it is a river, being the longest one in

Vermont, and navigable to ships of good size as far up as the Falls at Vergennes, eight miles, is noted in history. Here Arnold, when pressed by the pursuing British fleet, ran his flagship ashore and set her on fire, escaping with his crew overland to Crown Point. *Fort Cassin* stands at the mouth of the river and did good service in its day. It was in this river that Macdonough built and fitted out his fleet with which he won his noted victory of Plattsburg. But this river is not an easy one for a stranger to enter from the lake, and I would not advise a yachtsman to attempt it without a local pilot or in clear and quiet weather, when he might "feel" his way safely in.

South of this point I need give no direction, as the lake is open and clear of all dangerous places to Ticonderoga. It is, in fact, a continuous harbor, and all a skipper has to do is "not to sail into the fences," as the local saying is.

THE WEST SHORE, SAILING NORTH.

We will now begin to cruise northward.

Split Rock, once called, far more euphoniously, Cloven Rock, is a curiosity, and savants differ as to its origin. Historically it has been mistaken by many writers for *Mohawk Rock*, which stands in Burlington Bay. Historically there is no significance to Cloven Rock whatever, and it is interesting only as a curious freak of nature.

Whalon's Bay is immediately north of it, and is good for all winds save northerly ones. From these Gardiner Island, right opposite, is excellent mooring-ground.

Cruising northward, you come to *Essex*, where ample accommodation for yachts and yachtsmen will be found.

Bouquet River lies north of Essex some three miles. Here a sandbar stretches some one-half mile from its mouth. A yacht drawing six feet should give a good half-mile from the shore to be safe. Indeed, in cruising, no skipper should run in nearer than this distance between Cloven Rock and Willsborough Point, unless slowly feeling his way in on some quiet day. But, with this caution, a yacht has a free run from Cloven Rock until it comes to the Four Brothers, opposite Burlington, which we have already described.

SAILING NORTH FROM BURLINGTON ON THE
EAST SIDE OF THE LAKE.

Apple-Tree Shoals are two and one-fourth miles from the clubhouse, northwest, and are southeast from Apple-Tree Point, about three-fourths of a mile. Buoy on northwest corner. They stretch southeast from the buoy some forty rods. Depth of water five and a half feet.

Apple-Tree Point should be allowed one-eighth of a mile.

Winooski River enters the lake some two miles north of Apple-Tree Point. No yacht without pilot should seek to enter, I mean even small yachts, because of a wide deposit of sand that has been delivered into the lake from the river, and makes it inaccessible. In fact, this deposit of sand extends from Apple-Tree Point clean round to Colchester Point, and northward from Colchester Point two and a half miles farther. In cruising, no yacht should be carried within a line drawn from Apple-Tree Point to Colchester Point. It should be also borne in mind, in case of a southerly wind, that this is a bad lee shore and should be avoided.

Good fishing is found off the mouth of and in Winooski River. This river is a delightful one to boat on up to the rapids near Winooski village. There is no good reason to doubt that Champlain in his first exploration of the lake entered the Winooski and visited the falls; and it was doubtless from Lone Rock Point or Apple-Tree Point that his red associates pointed out to him the terrible Mohawk Rock, beyond which they must not go, unless with the utmost caution and prepared for attack.

In cruising from Burlington northward a yacht should, from Apple-Tree Point, lay its course to the west of *Colchester Shoals* until it commands a view of Cumberland Head. These shoals are buoyed on the northern point of them and extend from the buoy about one-half mile to the south and east of it. At low [1] water these shoals are visible, but at high water they are covered.

[1] We use the terms high and low water not in reference to any tide, of course, but to the fact that in the spring of the year the water in the lake is higher by some six or seven feet than it is later in the season. The depth of water as marked by us in these notes always refers to the depth when the water of the lake is at its *lowest* point.

Colchester Reef is northeast of the Shoals about three-fourths of a mile. It is a columnar rock of imposing height, and on its crest is a lighthouse. In pleasant or calm weather the rock can be approached safely by small boats. By an iron ladder visitors can reach the keeper's lodge, and from it a lovely view of the lake is obtainable.

Hog-Back Reef is half a mile to the northeast of the Light Station. It is buoyed. The buoy is on the northwest corner. The reef is not of large extent, and nearly if not quite visible at low water.

Hog-Back Island is north of this reef one-fourth of a mile, and east of this, stretching to the north two and a fourth miles, is the projection of Sandy Shoals, before alluded to.

We advise that in cruising all yachts keep to the west of Colchester Reef, unless under pilotage. Although there is a good passage between these several obstructions above mentioned to one who knows the waters, nevertheless, as there is little distance saved, it is better to stand out to the west of them all.

Jones Rock is north of Colchester Light

some two miles, due north. It is not buoyed, and has six feet of water on it.

Stave Island Ledge is one-half a mile north of this with five feet of water on it. No buoy.

Stave Island is one-half mile north of this.

Carlton Prize is three-fourths of a mile north. Due north of Stave Island and northwest of this, one-fourth of a mile, is *Providence Island*.

Between Stave Island and Providence Island is good depth of water, and no obstructions except Carlton's Prize (visible).

East of Providence Island and near to it is good anchorage against all winds.

Mallet's Bay is a lovely bit of water, and its shores are much frequented and admired. But off the entrance are the several reefs and shoals above mentioned, making it difficult of access to a stranger. We advise yachtsmen who desire to visit this beautiful section of the lake to take a pilot at Burlington for the cruise. The officers and local members of the Lake Champlain Yacht Club are always glad to assist visiting yachtsmen in every way, and good local pilots will be commended to them on application.

Providence Island is not only a good anchorage ground if caught in a squall or storm, but is provided with a hotel, and visitors will find not only accommodation as regular guests, but also supplies such as are needed on a cruise or in camp.

The outlet from the moorings at Providence Island going northward is a good one although not wide, and through it a yacht can pass to the north into wide waters free of all obstructions until it comes to

Sister Island Reef, one-fourth of a mile southeast of the South Sister Island. This reef is buoyed at the west end, is not large, and has good water on all sides.

South Sister Island is not to be approached either on the north or south of it very closely; and the same can be said of

North Sister Island, southeast of which are two bunches of rock (not buoyed), so that, in fact, a skipper should not sail either near to or between these islands unless perfectly familiar with the ground. If he is cruising to the north of the Gut, he should keep to the west of these islands, where he will find open water to Isle La

Motte, with the exception of Point au Roche Reef, previously mentioned. But if he is bound for St. Albans Bay, or Maquam Bay, or wishes to cruise down the east side of North Hero and must pass through the Gut, he should sail a course intermediate between Sister Islands and the shore of South Hero, which will bring him safely to the entrance of the Gut off Long Point.

From this point I decline to give farther direction, not wishing to take the responsibility. The passage of the Gut from Long Point to Knight's Point is a blind and crooked one and not to be attempted by a skipper unless familiar with the ground. In case of fair weather, light wind, and a small yacht, no doubt the passage might be threaded safely; but in case of a larger yacht or strong breeze or of a squall the passage, under any circumstances, is not an easy one to make, and unless under good pilotage should never be attempted. For this northern cruise, which in many respects is by far the most interesting one that the lake presents, all visiting yachtsmen would do well to put themselves in communication with the officers of the Champlain Yacht Club at Burlington, and through them obtain a competent pilot. This is the wise and safe course to pursue, and we earnestly commend it to all who sail Lake Champlain.

The Middle Reef — sailors know it as Bull Reef — is north of Sister Islands half a mile, and consists of two parts, South and North Bunch. There is good (narrow) water between them as there is good water between them and the North Hero shore, but the passage is narrow, and between the North Reef and North Hero shore not over one-fourth of a mile. In cruising north the course should be laid to the west of these islands and reefs. By doing this the run is made without obstructions from Providence Island to the south end of Isle La Motte, off the south end of which is

Hill's Island, between which and the shore is a small reef with only three feet of water, nearly midway between the island and Isle La Motte.

To the north of east, one-fourth of a mile from it, is a small reef with seven and a half feet on it, and to the southeast of Hill's Island half a mile distant is a reef (buoyed) with five feet on it.

Town's Reef is about three-fourths of a mile from Hill's Island, bearing nearly southeast (not buoyed by government, a private buoy may be on it in summer). It is some one-fourth of a mile from the shore of North Hero and about three-fourths of a mile southwest of Pelot's Point.

Horse-Shoe Shoal is equidistant between Isle La Motte and the entrance to Missisquoi Bay. It is a long, narrow shoal, stretching nearly north and south, about a mile long. It is *not buoyed* nor is it visible unless in exceptional circumstances and to good eyes. But by remembering that it lies nearly equidistant between the two shores, and that good water is on either side of it, it is not difficult to pass.

To the north of this is open water until you come to

Reynolds Point, where is the swinging bridge which is opened for the passage of crafts. From this point lay your course due north, bearing perhaps a trifle to the west for the dock at Rouse's Point, to which point we conducted you safely in our cruise down the western shore of the lake; and where, with flag honors, we leave you.

CRUISING EAST OF NORTH HERO.

Pelot's Point is the entrance to Missisquoi Bay from the western side of North Hero, and is opposite the southern portion of Isle La Motte. The entrance to the Alburgh Passage to the Bag, as it is called, is between Pelot's Point and Alburgh Point opposite, to the north, and is not difficult. There is a shoal (buoy on the south end) nearly equidistant between the two points, on which is seven feet of water. If the yacht draws more water than this, or over five feet, the course should be laid between the buoy and Pelot's Point to the south of it, a passage of good water about one-fourth of a mile in width.

Pelot's Bay lies within the mouth of the passage to the south, and is the mooring-ground of Mr. Saunders of Albany, N. Y., who has a fine summer camp on Pelot's Point, on the west side of the bay. In this bay is excellent mooring-ground, protected from all winds.

Alburg Passage is the narrow stretch of water lying between Alburg Tongue and North Hero, leading into Missisquoi Bay, and is free of obstructions until you come to the railroad bridge, where there is a draw. North of the draw a mile or more is the

Alburgh Hotel, or Alburgh Springs Hotel, which is so well and favorably known that I need not do more than thus mention it.

From this hotel the course bears north by east until you enter the main body of Missisquoi Bay, when the course curves to the east and south until you come to the famous

High-Gate Springs Hotel, located at the southern extremity of the bay, and whence you will naturally begin your return cruise, which can be by the same course you entered or through Maquam Bay and the large body of water east of North Hero.

There is no question but that the wide and long stretch of water east of the two Heroes is one of the most lovely and picturesque on Lake Champlain. It also abounds with fish, and by many is regarded as the best black-bass ground in the lake. It is beautifully studded with islands, and bounded with lovely shores, and should be visited by all yachtsmen and tourists. But we do not feel like attempting a verbal pilotage of this expanse of water, for fear that, trusting to it or encouraged to go beyond the courses marked out by us, some misadventure should happen. We earnestly recommend all to visit this delightful section of the lake, and at the same time as earnestly advise local pilotage until the visiting yachtsmen learn the water for themselves. As we have before said, the officers of the Lake Champlain Yacht Club at Burlington will gladly supply all needed information or assistance to all visitors seeking it.

PART IV.

HISTORICAL REMINISCENCES AND FACTS CONNECTED WITH THE SHORES OF LAKE CHAMPLAIN.

A QUARTER of a century has passed since my studentship of Lake Champlain and its shores began, and the farther my investigations were pushed the more was I astonished at the wealth of interesting material which lay scattered about on all sides, waiting to be collected and properly arranged for popular perusal. The period of time to be investigated in the interest of historical knowledge covers nearly three centuries, and during all these three hundred years there is not one of the multitude of events which have happened on this lake which has not been closely connected with, and had a more or less powerful influence upon, the course and development of American history. The destiny of Canada and the United States alike was decided by what occurred on its waters and shores, and yet no adequate examination into or presentation of these doings has ever been made by an American writer. The absence of such a statement as the subject demands seems to me to be a matter of such poignant regret as may not be felt or gauged by one unless he has given some attention to it and is measurably well informed in respect to the long and persistent struggle in which France and England engaged for the possession of the continent, and which, for the most part, was fought out on this lake.

It was my intention, in the closing section of this little volume, to have drawn at least a silhouette portrait of this momentous contest, that my readers might have a partial knowledge of what it meant to them: of its connection with American liberty and civilization, and how it made Lexington, Bunker Hill, Yorktown, free schools and free churches, possible. But my publisher cannot accommodate me with the space which the briefest possible presentation of the subject would require, and hence I must forego the attempt. It only remains for me to fill the few pages at my command with such

selections from a mass of notes and data I have
made and collected as seem most likely, in a
detached and disconnected form, to interest my
readers.   I imagine that to some — not the least
discerning — these abbreviated notes, jottings,
and memoranda of events, persons, and things
will make the most interesting and valuable
pages of this little book.

ARNOLD NOT AT TICONDEROGA WHEN CAPTURED
BY ETHAN ALLEN.

It is in the interest of the facts of history
that I record my conviction that Arnold was
not with Allen and his party at the capture
of Ticonderoga, and did not arrive there until
several days after its capture.   I am well aware
that Ira Allen, in his history of Vermont, and
Dr. Williams, state that Arnold, with a commission from Massachusetts as Colonel, arrived at
Castleton before Allen left there, and claimed of
Allen the right to supplant him in the command of the expedition, and that they state,
moreover, that he renewed the demand on the
morning of the 10th of May, when about to
attempt to enter the fortress.   Their statements

have been copied by nearly all historians since, and have been accepted as true by the people at large. Nevertheless, the statements of Ira Allen and Dr. Williams are directly contradicted by others, whose knowledge of the facts of the case and entire honesty cannot be successfully impeached, and especially by one whose word, were it not supported — as it is abundantly — by others, and by many corroborating circumstances, appears to me to be absolutely conclusive.

Nathan Beman was Allen's guide on that occasion. He was eighteen years of age, intelligent and honest. He had as a boy played with the children of the officers of the fort, and knew every nook and angle of it. It was because of his intimate knowledge of the fortress and the grounds around it, and his general intelligence, that he was selected by Allen for this responsible duty. From the circumstances of the case he was by Allen's side continuously. This Nathan Beman must have known the facts of the matter, and he always and repeatedly asserted, in the most positive manner, in after years, that Arnold did not

accompany the expedition, was not present with
the party on the night of the attack and
capture, and did not arrive at Ticonderoga till
several days after its capture. Beman's testimony was fully and often corroborated by many
others who had knowledge of the facts, nor did
Ethan Allen, in his account of the affair, make
the least mention of or allusion to Arnold as
being present until after the capture of the
fort. The fact seems to us as firmly established
as competent testimony can establish any fact
of history, that Benedict Arnold was not with
the expedition, and had no part whatever in
the capture of Ticonderoga.

WINOOSKI RIVER.

The Winooski River is not only a very beautiful stream, but to a peculiar degree historic.
The Abenakis Indians originally occupied the
east side of the lake from opposite Mohawk
Rock to the northern end of Missisquoi Bay,
and the Winooski River was, because of its
multitude of salmon and the beauty of its banks,
a favorite resort of theirs. It was along this
river also that the old Indian trail ran which

led over to the Connecticut, and was much used
by all the northern tribes in friendship with
the Abenakis, in their annual migrations to and
from the seacoast. The Indians and French
alike used this route in their forays against the
English settlements in western Massachusetts.
It was down this river that the captives taken
at Deerfield were brought in the winter of 1704,
on their fearful journey to Canada. There is
no section in New England more interesting to
those who are curious as to ancient times and
early colonial matters than that which lies
between Burlington Bay and Missisquoi Bay.
The Abenakis were not only a brave tribe, but
a large and most ancient one. The famous Urn
in the Museum of the University is believed to
be of their manufacture, and its artistic excellence is of such high order as to provoke curiosity as to the origin of this ancient people,
and the development of manufacture among
them. At the mouth of the La Moille River
they evidently had a large and permanent en-
campment, for many graves have been discovered there in which the skeletons exhumed
were found to have been buried in a sitting

posture, facing westward, and in these were
many aboriginal relics finished with great perfection. The whole region is of interest to
antiquarians.

IRA ALLEN.

Ira Allen was the youngest of six sons, and
was born in Cornwall, Ct., April 21, 1751.
His brother, Ethan Allen, was the first-born,
and became more noted in the annals of the
times from the accident of age and circumstance rather than from superior ability; for Ira
Allen, in many respects, outranked him in
mental capacity, especially as applied to the
management of commercial affairs. The services he rendered the State of Vermont. which,
in fact, he organized — for no one could claim
that the timid and slow-moving Chittenden was
anything more than a figurehead in the spirited
movements and audacious negotiations of the
time — were of the highest order. Allowing
that he was subtle to a degree, at times an intri-
gant to the verge of disloyalty, and unduly
moved by personal and selfish considerations, it
should nevertheless be remembered that in these

characteristics he simply reflected the fashion of
the times and the habits of the men with whom
he was associated.   Surrounded by sharpers, it
is not to be wondered at if he became at times
and in certain connections a sharper himself.
The Allens were not saints, and Ira, like his
brothers, would not, we presume, by a conclave
of angels, have been selected for canonization.
But his faults were largely those of nature, and
his failings such as were shared with him by
the best of his associates.   The leading spirits
that with their shrewdness and their courage,
out of fourfold opposition, hewed the State of
Vermont, were nearly all born in Connecticut
and New Hampshire, which is the same as
saying that they were "on the make," and
had little scruple how they made it, if within
the law.   And as at first there was no law
save such as their ambition dictated and their
rifles enforced, they did pretty much as they
pleased.   To them the valley of Champlain was
as the promised land to the Israelites, and
they went in to possess it, and they did !

It should be remembered that Ethan Allen
was taken prisoner soon after the commence-

ment of the Revolutionary War, and was carried a captive to England. Remember Baker — probably the most able of the group — was killed at Isle la Noix by an Indian. Seth Warner joined the Continental army, as also did others of prominence — so that Thomas Chittenden and Ira Allen were left in absolute control of public affairs. These two men were, to all intents and purposes, *dictators*. Allen was by far the stronger spirit and of more brilliant parts. His physical appearance was unusually attractive; his address pleasing, and his manners those of a gentleman. In counsel he was astute, and in action bold; to the ability and courage of his family was, in his case, added suavity; the smooth suavity of a natural born diplomat. His mind was capable of large conceptions, and his disposition was generous. He was public-spirited to a degree, especially where his own interests were coincident with those of the public.

As a city, Burlington owes to him its early prominence, and the university which crowns its site, its existence and location. It was his hand that drew the memorial to the Legislature one hundred years ago — 1789 — which secured for it the assistance of the State and its location at Burlington. He accompanied the memorial with a subscription of .£4,000.

At this time, Ira Allen was one of the richest men in the country. He owned three hundred thousand acres of land on the shore of the lake. His immense domain stretched from Ferrisburg to the Canada line, and included the most desirable land of eleven townships. To me, having knowledge of the territory embraced, the magnificent forests standing on it, the immense fisheries with which it abounded, the marble quarries it contained, the wealth of its soils, and the majestic scenery which distinguished it, it was the most magnificent estate ever owned by one individual in a civilized community on the globe.

Of the misfortunes that befell him in later years; of the injustice he experienced, and the miseries he endured; how he was robbed of reputation and property; how his liberty even was threatened, and to escape unjust imprisonment he was compelled to fly the State he had created, may not be written here. The wrongs and misfortunes of Ira Allen, on the eastern side

of the lake, and of William Gilliland, on the
shore directly opposite, are the direst I ever
read of inflicted on deserving men, under form
of law, in a civilized community. It is enough
to say that the man whose wisdom and courage
created Vermont; whose diplomacy preserved
it from devastation by the British; whose foresight made the victory at Bennington possible
to American arms; whose public spirit and gen-
erosity erected its university, and who, by his
ability in business, became its wealthiest citizen,
died in exile and poverty, and was buried by
charity in an unknown grave. And, stranger
than all, there is not within the borders of
Vermont a monument or even a tablet erected
to his memory!

THE BOUQUET RIVER.

By one event this little and little-known
stream is lifted into historic prominence, and
is connected with famous measures and men; an
event which brought the attention of Europe to
its banks, and profoundly stirred the humane
emotions of mankind. It is strange that a spot
should be forgotten on which an act was done,

only 122 years ago, of so horrible a nature that
it awoke the thunders of Chatham's eloquence,
and filled with horror the bosom of the Christian
world; an act which harmonized the popular
factions in the American colonies and united
them in one common impulse of indignation and
rage against the host of Burgoyne at Saratoga.
It seems fitting that I should rescue from forgetfulness the act which made the Bouquet
noted throughout a hemisphere, and will forever make it noted in the history of the
continent.

Previous to his advance, Burgoyne had sent
out a summons to the Indians to meet him at
the falls of the Bouquet. The result was that
they obeyed him in such numbers and animated
with such ferocity that he was alarmed, and
filled with forebodings as to the issue of his own
act. It was June 20, 1777, that he convened
the chiefs in council. The council was held
about half a mile below the house of William
Gilliland. Burgoyne addressed them and in-
vited them to join him in his campaign against
the Americans. A chief—chosen to represent
the assembled tribes—accepted the invitation

in a speech of such eloquence and ferocity that it startled the English officers — for in it he pledged his kindred to a merciless warfare against the colonies. The treaty was ratified with savage orgies, and England stood condemned for enlisting wild hordes of savages as her allies in a contest against men of her own blood and civilization. What a subject this famous council and the influences of it would make for a historic poem or romance!

BATEAUX.

These boats are constantly mentioned, not only in the early records of military operations on the lake, but as supplying the settlers with their principal means of transportation in times of peace. They were not only in use upon Champlain, but also upon the Hudson and the Mohawk. We have often been asked what was the fashion of these popular and most serviceable craft? To this interrogation the correct answer is — that they were long narrow boats with flat bottoms. They were from six to twelve feet in width, and from sixteen to thirty feet in length. As a rule, they were not decked over, but some had a partial deck and a cabin at the stern. They were propelled by oars and sails both. In shallow water they were pushed along by poles. They drew, even when loaded, but a foot or so of water, and running before a good wind sailed quite fast. I have seen the large bateaux on the St. Lawrence, with their immense square sails, running before the wind, outsail the crack yachts of the Canadians.

THE BOUQUET is a picturesque and beautiful river. Its source is among the Adirondacks, and its course a long and crooked one. It flows into the lake at Willsborough. It may have been named after General Bouquet, or from the multitude of flowers which in spring and summer adorned its banks, or from *bouquet*, the French word for flume or trough, which term is descriptive of the appearance of the river below the falls. At these falls the original settlement of William Gilliland, Esq., was made. This remarkable and noted man was the great pioneer of the western shore of Champlain. His history, in its vicissitudes, struggles, wrongs, and forlorn death, surpasses the creations of the

wildest romance.   The Bouquet and Willsborough are well worth visiting, if for no other
object than in respect to the memory of the
noble and unhappy man who first selected its
lovely banks for his home. (See note on William Gilliland.)   A part of General Burgoyne's
fleet entered the Bouquet, and British gunboats
bombarded and captured Willsborough village
during the War of 1812.

THE FOUR BROTHERS — or *Iles de Quatre
Vents*, The Islands of the Four Winds, as the
French named them — are a beautiful group of
islands, and should be visited by all tourists of
the lake.   The French gave characteristic and
vividly descriptive names to physical objects and
geographical peculiarities.   They were excelled
only by the aboriginals in this respect.   The
English had less imagination and poetry in their
make-up, and hence their nomenclature is puerile
or vulgar.   Their rude displacement of French
and Indian names was a misfortune to the
country.   I cannot better illustrate this than
by reminding the reader, as his eyes dwell upon
one of the loftiest peaks of the Green Moun-

tains, that the French called it *"Lion Couchant"* —a noble appellation. The English looked at the same sublime formation and called it "Camel's Rump!" a damnable name. It has since been "improved" by us Americans into *"Camel's Hump."* Ye gods, what a name for such a noble mountain! I pray you, reader, help me to popularize the old French appellation of "The Crouching Lion."

FISH AND FISHING.

The abundance of fish in Lake Champlain when its shores were first settled was a matter of surprise to the settlers. The records that were made at that time by honest and honorable men, while they stir astonishment, nevertheless are above impeachment. It is doubtful if any body of water on the continent was ever visited by such vast numbers of salmon as Champlain once was. The rivers flowing into the lake were as thick with them, at times, as are the rivers of the Pacific coast to-day. It was dangerous to attempt to ride a spirited horse through them because of the multitude of salmon that actually packed the water. As late as 1823, *fifteen hundred pounds* were taken at Chesterfield, at one haul of the seine. They were taken in great quantities at Plattsburg in 1824–25. Civilization has its triumphs, it is true, but what a pity that it achieves them at the cost of such a vast destruction. If the lake had the fish to-day that it had even fifty years ago, it would bring millions of dollars to the two States that border its waters.

CLOVEN ROCK.

It is a pity that the name "Split" has been allowed to fix itself to this singular and picturesque formation. The French called it *Roche rendu,* and its original name in English was Cloven Rock. May I ask that pilots, correspondents, and tourists assist me to restore to it its old-time appropriate name? Cloven Rock contains considerable surface, and is separated from the promontory near it by a fissure some ten feet wide. Much exaggeration is indulged in by makers of "guide-books" touching this physical curiosity, especially as to the depth of the fissure; some stating that it goes down *five hundred feet!* the fact being it doesn't go *down* at all. For at low water the tourist can walk through the fissure on solid rock and *dry* rock at that ! But who expects facts in a guide-book ?

ESSEX, originally called Elizabeth, was named by William Gilliland, the original proprietor of the site of the village, after his wife. Elizabethtown is not to be confounded with it, although named by the same party and for the same reason. Mr. Gilliland designated many places within the limits of his immense possessions by the names of members of his family.

CRAB ISLAND was originally called St. Michael's Island. After Macdonough's battle, it was called Hospital Island, because those who were wounded in that fight, whether American or English, were landed there for treatment.

VALCOUR ISLAND is in New York State, and is the largest island in the lake belonging to that State. It is a most interesting spot, historically considered. Between it and the western shore, Arnold fought his desperate fight with Carleton. On the east side Amherst cap-

tured the French bateaux fleeing from Crown
Point toward Canada, and thus extinguished forever the French possession of and title to the
lake. To the northeast of the same island,
Macdonough won his famous victory.

THE LA MOILLE RIVER. — This river was undoubtedly entered by Champlain in 1609. It
was called by him *La Mouette,* or Gull River,
because this species of birds were very plentiful
at its mouth. In Charlevoix's map of 1744, it
is written La Rivière à la Mouelle, this change
from Champlain's nomenclature being due un-
questionably to a failure on the part of the writ-
ing clerk to cross the two *t*'s. The transition
from La Mouelle to La Moille is an easy one.
In this case a blunder is acceptable, because
La Moille is a pleasant word, but I confess to a
wish that the name Champlain gave it may be
preserved and popularized, and that we might
still know it as he knew it — as *La Mouette.*

HISTORIC SITES.

I presume that all who have knowledge of the
route would unhesitatingly admit that the
journey by water from New York up the Hud-

son, and through the Whitehall Canal to Lake Champlain, and down the lake to Rouse's Point, would bring the voyager in view of more lovely and majestic scenery and memorable historic sites than any other tour of equal length that might be taken on the continent. For on this voyage he would pass West Point and old Fort Orange — now Albany — and in sight of the very spot where stood the tree to which Putnam was bound to be tortured in 1757; Forts Edward and Miller — near the former of which Miss McCrea was murdered. He would pass near the spot where General Burgoyne surrendered his sword, October 17, 1777, and where the brave Frazier fell. Farther on is the South Bay of Lake Champlain, where General Dieskau landed his forces in his vain attempt to capture General Johnson's army on Lake George. Then he would come to the world-renowned ruins of Ticonderoga, and a little farther on to Crown Point, where the French, in 1731, built Fort St. Frederick, and, later, General Amherst, in 1759, began the magnificent fortress that was captured from the English by Colonel Seth Warner, the day after Ethan Allen seized, with his band

of Green Mountain boys, Ticonderoga. At
Valcour Island, he beholds the scene of the
brave naval fight Arnold made with the English
fleet, and, to the east of the same island, the
spot where the English gunboats, under Amherst,
captured the last boats to bear the French flag
on the lake, as they were fleeing northward
after they had evacuated Crown Point. Between
this island and Cumberland Head, he sails over
water where the brave Macdonough won his
great victory against his equally brave but less
fortunate antagonist — one of the fiercest con-
flicts ever fought by ships on any water. While
at the Isle La Motte, he can still see the mounds
that mark the spot where once stood Fort St.
Anne — the first fort built on the lake, and
around whose walls was the first settlement
ever made by civilized men in the State of
Vermont or on the lake. For Fort Anne was
built in 1665, while the little fort on Chimney
Point was erected in 1690, and old Fort Dummer — a mere block house — on the west bank
of the Connecticut, was put up in 1724. Is it
not a strange thing that so few Americans have
ever gone over this course, unequalled as it

is for the beauty of its scenery, and the multitude of its historic sites and inspiring memories ?

VERGENNES

Is a most interesting locality. Although in respect to its population it is but a village, and not a large one at that, it, nevertheless, is one of the oldest cities in the United States, for it was incorporated October 23, 1788. By its ancient charter of incorporation it is four hundred and eighty by four hundred rods in extent. Its first mayor was elected March 12, 1789. He was Enoch Woodbridge, subsequently chief justice of the Supreme Court. In 1798, a State-house was erected here, and in that year the General Assembly held its session in it.

The first settler was Donald McIntosh, a native of Scotland. He fought in the battle of Culloden. He emigrated to this country with General Wolfe's army, and died July 14, 1803, aged eighty-four years. Otter River passes through the city, and its falls give abundant power for manufacturing purposes. During the war this power was utilized far more than it is now. The river is navigable to the foot of the falls, some seven miles from the lake, for vessels of large draft. It was here that Macdonough fitted out his fleet with which he won his celebrated victory against the English off Plattsburg. It has an excellent hotel, and is one of the prettiest villages on the shore of the lake. Tourists would find the sail up the river and a stroll through this little old city most enjoyable.

TICONDEROGA.

That the reader may have certain momentous events in close sequence and easily memorized, I would note, —

That the skirmish at Lexington occurred April 19, 1775.

Ethan Allen, with his band of followers, captured Ticonderoga May 10, 1775.

Seth Warner captured the fortress at Crown Point the next day.

In these forts they found more than two hundred pieces of cannon, some mortars, howitzers, and an immense amount of military stores, and beside these a large quantity of ship and boat building material. Soon after, the only armed sloop on the lake was captured at St. Johns. And thus at the very beginning of the Revolutionary War, Lake Champlain, with all its power and prestige, and which had cost England half a century to capture, passed into the hands of the patriots. Many of the cannon captured at Ticonderoga were drawn by ox-teams to Boston, and enabled General Washington to make good his works on Dorchester Heights.

THE EARLY HISTORY OF VERMONT.

As a matter of interest to the younger readers of these pages, I make the following epitomized statement of facts relating to Vermont before she became a State.

The tract of unoccupied mountainous territory which lay in 1749 between Connecticut River and Lake Champlain was then claimed by both the provinces of New Hampshire and New York. Both, of course, were English provinces and under royal governors. In that year the governor of New Hampshire began to make grants to individuals and town charters to organized bodies. The governor of New York was greatly incensed at this proceeding of

his rival, and carried the matter to the king in
England. In 1764, it was decided by him that
all the territory west of the Connecticut and
east of the St. Lawrence, on a line drawn
through Lake Champlain, belonged to the
Province of New York. But during these
sixteen years, before the matter was thus decided, the governor of New Hampshire had
made *one hundred and thirty-six grants* to *bonâ-
fide* settlers, chiefly to men of character and
means from Massachusetts, Rhode Island, and
Connecticut. These "grants" thus given (sold)
to these settlers by the governor of New Hampshire, the governor of New York pronounced
null and void, and summoned said settlers to
purchase new titles to their land of him. Un-
fortunately, he fixed the price at a very high
figure. Some of the towns complied with his
demand, but the majority refused to pay twice
over for their lands. This is why what is now
Vermont was originally called "New Hampshire Grants," and how they were brought into
a contest with New York, which lasted a quarter
of a century, and was of a most bitter character.

The governor of New York acted with great energy, not to say cruelty, in the matter; for he proceeded to grant the lands which the settlers would not repurchase, to others, and actions of ejectment were brought, and judgment obtained against them in the Albany courts. The settlers on the grants were thus compelled either to surrender the lands they had paid for and the houses they had built and the improvements they had made, or resist these unjust proceedings against them. As they were brave men, they naturally decided on the latter course, and when the New York officers came among them to eject them from their possessions by force, they resisted them with arms. Many of these officers were roughly handled, and treated to flagellations more or less severe; whence arose the term "Beech Seal," viz., if a sheriff had the "Beech Seal" put upon him, it meant that he had been publicly whipped. The grim humor of the term was fully appreciated, no doubt, by one of the parties to the transaction, at least. It is to the honor of the militia of New York to record that they refused to be parties to the attempt to enforce so unjust a decision.

It was amid such scenes and in defence of
the rights of the settlers that Ethan Allen
came into prominence. He was born in Connecticut and came of good stock. With him
and with equal spirit stood Remember Baker,
who was born in Connecticut also. No bolder
men ever lived; nor were they lacking in education or sagacity. These two rallied their fellow-
settlers to the contest, and devised measures for
the common welfare. In 1774 the governor of
New York caused an act to be passed to the
effect that unless the offenders surrendered
themselves to the authorities of that province
within seventy days they should be indicted in
a court of that colony for a capital offence, and,
if convicted, should suffer death without benefit
of clergy. At the same time a proclamation
was issued offering a reward of fifty pounds for
the apprehension of Ethan Allen, Seth Warner,
and six others. This embittered the feeling of
the settlers, and the conflict grew hotter and
hotter until the breaking out of the war
between Great Britain and the colonies put a
stop to the controversy for the time being. As

histories of the time, as I may not extend this note to greater length.

THE FIRST SETTLEMENT IN VERMONT.

As there has been much difference in the statements of local historians as to when and where the first settlement by white men was made in Vermont, we will record the following facts:—

Fort Dummer was built in 1724, and was located in the present town of Brattleboro — at the south-east corner of it. It was an ordinary block house built of logs, and not of large size. It was strictly a military post and not a settlement in the proper sense of the word.

In 1690 (March 26) Captain Jacobus de Warm was sent from Albany with a small body of men to build a fort at the narrows of the lake, near what afterward was known as Crown Point. He built a small stone fort at what is now Chimney Point, in the town of Addison.

From this it appears that the settlement at Chimney Point in the town of Addison was made *thirty-four years* earlier than the one made in Brattleboro.

The third fact is that the French built Fort
St. Anne, afterward named, from the officer who
constructed it, Fort La Motte, upon the Isle La
Motte, in the year 1665. Of this there is and
can be no question. It therefore appears that
the settlement on Isle La Motte was made
twenty-five years before that at Chimney Point,
and fifty-nine years before Fort Dummer was
built on the Connecticut, at Brattleboro. The
location of this old fort, which, were it now
standing, would be over two centuries old, can
still be traced by discernible mounds, on one of
which stands a white pine over six feet in diameter. The Isle La Motte is regarded by many
as the most beautiful one in the lake.

CHAMPLAIN AT BURLINGTON.

Hon. Thomas H. Canfield, several years since,
made a very exhaustive canvass of the facts
bearing upon this question, and a written
presentation of them, as brought out by
this examination. Indeed his article is one
of the clearest in point of style, and valuable
as viewed in the light of material collected,
of all the numberless ones that have been pre-

pared by native writers, for it includes not only
the evidences which go to prove that Champlain
entered the Winooski, but a vast amount of information concerning the early navigation of
the lake, and many other interesting matters
associated with it. Without entering into a
full exposition of my views touching Champlain's visit to the vicinity of Burlington Bay,
I beg to state that there is no reason to think
that he did not enter the Winooski, while there
exists the strongest evidence to prove that he
did. It is in his own record that he entered
the La Moille River — Rivière de la Mouette or
Gull River, as he called it — and, from inference,
it follows that he would not pass the Winooski
without entering it also. I make no doubt but
that he went up the Winooski as far as the
falls, and that he visited Burlington Bay, getting
his first view of it, probably, from some point
between what is now the park and the railway
tunnel. From this point he could clearly dis-
cern the mountains to the south and west on the
western shore, — as he says in his journal he did,
— which he could not do from any other point
so clearly unless it may have been from Apple-

Tree Point. From one of these two positions he undoubtedly got his first glimpses of Mohawk Rock, of which and its significance as marking the boundary line between the United People and the northern Indians he must have been repeatedly told by his savage associates from the hour they first entered the lake. His allusion also to " groves of chestnut-trees " fixes, conclusively, the fact of his presence in this locality, for it is well known that the chestnut-tree was not indigenous on the western shore of the lake to a point so far north, while it is well established that large groves of chestnut-trees were standing on the eastern side of the lake at least as far north as the La Moille River.

SOURCE OF MODERN SOILS.

The rich soils of the Champlain Valley, which to-day are so productive under cultivation, are accounted for by the geological fact that, at not a very remote period, much of it was under ocean water. The shells of mollusks are found in abundance in the clays and sand several hundred feet above the present water level. The bones of the whale now in the State Museum were discovered sixty feet above the level of the lake. These rich soils, which are the source of modern agricultural wealth, were — geologically speaking — recently covered with the waters of the ocean, and were permanently enriched thereby. Portions of Chittenden, Addison, Rutland, and Franklin counties, and the whole of Grand Isle, share the benefits of this creative cause.

WILD GAME.

It is comparatively but recent that wild game both of animals and birds were unusually plenty on Lake Champlain and its shores. As noted in another place in this volume, salmon were exceedingly plenty in the Saranac and other rivers flowing into the lake, as late as 1824. Among birds the wild pigeons were so plenty in the forests around it as to be beyond estimation. The old records and diaries are filled with mention of them, and bear ample testimony of the astonishment with which their numbers filled the minds of the early settlers. In one of the towns the following record is to be found:

"The number of pigeons is immense. Twenty-five nests are often found on one tree. Acres of such trees are to be seen anywhere. For hundreds of acres the ground underneath them is covered with their droppings to the depth of two inches. Their noise in the evening and at night is so troublesome that people cannot sleep. When the young are grown to a suitable size, just before they are ready to fly, it is common for the settlers to cut down the trees and gather a horse-load in a few minutes."

THE BEAVER.

Among the wild animals once exceedingly numerous on the shores of Lake Champlain were the otter and beaver. The one family gave its name to the longest river in the State, and the other were not only very numerous but were noted among dealers in peltry for their size and the high quality of their fur. These extraordinary animals have been banished the larger part of the continent, and it is a rarity to see one even in the menageries and the gardens of natural history. Only a few sportsmen even, probably of my generation, have ever been so

placed as to study the habits of these extraordinary animals; and those of the generation that
are to succeed us will doubtless never be able by
any amount of journeying within the limits of
the country to become personally acquainted
with them.   These facts suggest to me the value
of a note that shall preserve, in the best possible
form of expression, the knowledge of the characteristics and the habits of an animal the capture of which has given such wide employment
to commerce, assisted pioneer life in its development, and given to taste and wealth one of the
most beautiful coverings ever made for human
use.   I do not propose to trust my own knowledge in describing this animal, but will tran-
scribe the best description I have ever read
of the beaver, as written by one of the early
settlers of Vermont, who was not only a scholar
but a naturalist of such gifts and attainments
as few men enjoy.   I refer to Doctor Samuel
Williams, LL.D.   The following is his description of the beaver; and beyond what he has
written there is nothing to be said of the animal.

"The American beaver is between three and
four feet in length, and weighs from forty to sixty

pounds. His head is like that of a rat, inclined to
the earth; his back rises in an arch between his
head and tail. His teeth are long, broad, strong,
and sharp. Four of these, two in the upper
and two in the under jaw, are called *incisors*.
These teeth project one or two inches beyond
the jaw, and are sharp, and curved like a car-
penter's gouge. In his fore feet the toes are
separate, as if designed to answer the purposes
of fingers and hands. His hind feet are accom-
modated with webs, suited to the purpose of
swimming. His tail is a foot long, an inch
thick, and five or six inches broad. It is covered with scales, and with a skin similar to that
of a fish.

"In no animal does the *social instinct and habit*
appear more strong or universal than in the
beaver. Wheresoever a number of these animals are found, they immediately associate and
combine in society, to pursue their common
business and welfare. Everything is done by
the united counsels and labors of the whole
community. Their societies are generally collected together in the months of June and July;
and their numbers when thus collected frequently

amount to two or three hundred; all of which immediately engage in a joint effort to promote the common business and safety of the whole society; apparently acting under a common inclination and direction. When the beaver is found in a solitary state, he appears to be a timid, inactive, and stupid animal. Instead of attempting any important enterprise, he contents himself with digging a hole in the earth for safety and concealment. His genius seems to be depressed, his spirits broken, and everything enterprising is lost in an attention to personal safety; but he never loses his natural instinct to find or form a pond.[1] When combined in society, his disposition and powers assume their natural direction, and are exerted to the highest advantage. Everything is then undertaken which the beaver is capable of performing.

"The society of beavers seems to be *regulated and governed* altogether by natural dispositions and laws. Their society, in all its pursuits and

---

[1] A young beaver was tamed in the southern part of this State. He became quite inoffensive, and without any disposition to depart, but was most of all pleased when he was at work forming a dam in a small stream near the house.

operations, appears to be a society of peace and
mutual affection, guided by one principle, and
under the same direction. No contention, dis-
agreement, contrary interests or pursuits, are
ever seen among them; but perfect harmony
and agreement prevails through their whole
dominions. The principle of this union and
regulation is not the superior strength, art, or
activity of any individual. Nothing has the
appearance, among them, of the authority or influence of a chief or leader. Their association
and management have the aspect of a pure and
perfect democracy, founded on the principle of
perfect equality, and the strongest mutual
attachment. This principle seems to be sufficient to preserve the most perfect harmony, and
to regulate all the proceedings of their largest
societies.

" When these animals are collected together,
their first attention is to *the public business and
affairs* of the society to which they belong.
The beavers are amphibious animals, and must
spend one part of their time in the water and
another upon the land. In conformity to this
law of their natures, their first employment is

to find a situation convenient for both these
purposes.   With this view, a lake, a pond, or a
running stream of water is chosen for the scene
of their habitation and future operations.   If
it be a lake or a pond that is selected, the water
is always of such depth that the beavers may
have sufficient room to swim under the ice, and
one of which they can have an entire and undisturbed possession.   If a stream of water is
chosen, it is always such a stream as will form a
pond that shall be every way convenient for
their purpose.   And such is their foresight and
comprehension of these circumstances, that they
never form an erroneous judgment, or fix upon
a situation that will not answer their designs and
convenience.   Their next business is to construct
a dam.   This is always chosen in the most convenient part of the stream; and the form of it
is either direct, circular, or with angles, as the
situation and circumstances of the water and
land require; and so well chosen are both the
place and the form of these dams, that no engi-
neer could give them a better situation and
form either for convenience, strength, or dura-
tion.   The materials of which the dams are

constructed are wood and earth. If there be a
tree on the side of the river, which would
naturally fall across the stream, several of the
beavers set themselves, with great diligence, to
cut it down with their teeth. Trees to the big-
ness of twenty inches diameter are thus thrown
across a stream. They next gnaw off the
branches from the trunk, that the tree may
assume a level position. Others, at the same
time, are cutting down smaller trees and saplings from one to ten inches diameter. These
are cut into equal and convenient lengths.
Some of the beavers drag these pieces of wood
to the side of the river, and others swim with
them to the place where the dam is to be built.
As many as can find room are engaged in sink-
ing one end of these stakes, and as many more
in raising, fixing, and securing the other end.
While many of the beavers are thus laboring
upon the wood, others are equally engaged in
carrying on the earthen part of the work.
The earth is brought in their mouths, formed
into a kind of mortar with their feet and tails,
and spread over the vacancies between the
sticks. Saplings and the small branches of

trees are twisted and worked up with the mud
and slime, until all the vacancies are filled up,
and no crevice is left in any part of the work
for the water to find a passage through. The
magnitude and extent of the dams, which the
beavers thus construct, is much larger than we
should imagine was possible to be effected by
such laborers or instruments. At the bottom,
the dam is from six to twelve feet thick ; at the
top it is generally two or three feet in width.
In that part of the dam which is opposed to the
current, the stakes are placed obliquely ; but on
that side where the water is to fall, the stakes
are placed in a perpendicular direction, and the
dam assumes the same form and position as the
stakes. The extent of these works is from fifty
to a hundred feet in length, and always of
such a height as to effect the purposes they
have in view. The ponds which are formed by
these dams are of all dimensions, from four or
five to five or six hundred acres. They are generally spread over lands abounding with trees and
bushes of the softest wood, maple, birch, alder,
poplar, willow, etc. The better to preserve
their dams, the beavers always leave sluices or

passages near the middle for the redundant waters to pass off. These sluices are generally about eighteen inches in width and depth, and as many in number as the waters of the stream generally require.

" When the public works are completed, their *domestic concerns and affairs* next engage their attention. The dam is no sooner completed, than the beavers separate into small bodies, to build cabins, or houses for themselves. These houses are built upon piles, along the borders of the pond. They are of an oval form, resembling the construction of an haycock; and they vary in their dimensions, from four to ten feet in diameter, according to the number of families they are designed to accommodate. They are always of two stories, generally of three, and sometimes they contain four. Their walls are from two to three feet in thickness, at the bottom; and are formed of the same material as the dams. They rise perpendicularly a few feet, then assume a curved form, and terminate in a dome or vault, which answers the purpose of a roof. These edifices are built with much solidity, and neatness. On the inward side, they are smooth, but rough on the outside; always impenetrable to the rain, and of sufficient strength to resist the most impetuous winds. The lower story is about two feet high: the second story has a floor of sticks, covered with mud: the third story is divided from the second, in the same manner, and terminated by the roof raised in the form of an arch. Through each floor, there is a communication; and the upper floor is always above the level of the water, when it is raised to its greatest height. Each of these huts has two doors; one, on the land side, to enable them to go out and procure provisions by land; another under the water, and below where it freezes, to preserve their communication with the pond. If this at any time begins to be covered with ice, the ice is immediately broken, that the communication may not be cut off with the air.

"In these huts, the *families* of the beavers have their residence. The smallest of their cabins contain one family, consisting generally of five or six beavers; and the largest of the buildings will contain from twenty to thirty. No society of animals can ever appear better regulated, or more happy, than the family of beavers. The male and the female always pair. Their selection is not a matter of chance, or accident; but appears to be derived from taste, and mutual affection. In September, the happy couple lay up their store of provisions, for winter. This consists of bark, the tender twigs of trees, and various kinds of soft wood. When their provisions are prepared, the season of love and repose commences: and during the winter they remain in their cabins, enjoying the fruits of their labours, and partaking in the sweets of domestic happiness. Towards the end of winter, the females bring forth their young, to the number of three or four. Soon after, the male retires to gather fish, and vegetables, as the spring opens; but the mother remains at home, to nurse and rear up the offspring, until they are able to follow their dams. The male occasionally returns, but not to tarry, until the fall of the year. But if any injury is done to their public works, the whole society are soon collected, and join all their forces to repair the injury, which affects their commonwealth.

"Nothing can exceed *the peace and regularity*

which prevails in the families, and through the whole commonwealth of these animals. No discord or contention ever appears in any of their families. Every beaver knows his own apartment, and store house; and there is no pilfering or robbing from one another. The male and the female are mutually attached to, and never prove unfriendly, or desert one another. Their provisions are collected, and expended, without any dissension. Each knows its own family, business, and property; and they are never seen to injure, oppose, or interfere with one another. The same order and tranquillity prevail through the commonwealth. Different societies of beavers never make war upon one another, or upon any other animals. When they are attacked by their enemies, they instantly plunge into the water, to escape their pursuit: and when they cannot escape, they fall an easy sacrifice.

" In the *arts* necessary for their safety, the beavers rise to great eminence. The situation, direction, form, solidity, beauty, and durability of their dams, are equal to anything of the kind, which has ever been performed by man. They

always form a right judgment, which way the
tree will fall ; and when it is nearly cut down,
they appoint one of their number, to give notice
by a stroke of his tail, when it begins to fall.
With their tails, they measure the lengths of
their dams, of the stakes they are to use, of a
breach that is made in their works, and of the
length of the timber that is necessary to repair
it. When an enemy approaches their dominions,
the beaver which makes the discovery, by strik-
ing on the water with his tail, gives notice to
the whole village of the approaching danger;
and all of them instantly plunge into the
water.   And when the hunters are passing
through their country, some of their number
appear to be sentinels, to give notice of their
approach.

   " The colour of the beaver is different, according to the different climates, which they inhabit.   In the most northern parts, they are
generally black ; in Vermont they are brown;
and their color becomes lighter as we approach
towards the south.   Their fur is of two sorts,
all over their bodies.   That which is longest, is
generally about an inch long, but on the back

it sometimes extends to two inches, gradually
shortening towards the head and tail. This
part is coarse, and of little use. The other part
of the fur consists of a very fine and thick
down, about three quarters of an inch long, so
soft that it feels like silk, and is that which is
used in manufactories. Castor, of so much use
in medicine, is produced from the body of the
beaver. It is contained in four bags, in the
lower belly.

"The largest of these animals, of which I
have any certain information, weighed sixty-
three pounds and an half; but it is only in a
situation remote from, and undisturbed by the
frequent appearances of men, that they attain
their greatest magnitude, or their highest perfection of society. The beaver has deserted all
the southern parts of Vermont, and is now to
be found only in the most northern and uncul-
tivated parts of the State."

VERMONT MARBLES.

Among all the ornamental stones used in
architecture, either ancient or modern, not one
is more prized by wealth, knowledge, and taste,

than marble; and in no place on the globe has
nature made so extensive and rich a deposit as
along the eastern shore of Lake Champlain.
Here she has placed the purest white and the
dunnest black, the blue, the gray, the rose and
pink, almost side by side. Between the white
and black over forty shades are grouped. Every
color and tint required for interior embellish-
ment, from the delicate shade of the sea-pink
shell to the flaming splendor of sapphire, from
snow to jet; the neutral grays, the cerulean
blues, the mottled, the veined, the composite;
all are here. What unchiselled vases, what
unhewn statues, what unshaped monuments,
what dormant shafts and unraised columns,
what mansions, palaces, and sovereign capitols,
are lying unbuilded on the shores of Lake Champlain, awaiting the word that shall shape them
to fit proportion, and set them to be admired of
all and stand until they crumble, in the light of
day!

The development of the marble industry in
Vermont might have been far more rapid than
it has been, and, vast as it now is, much more
so, had it not been for that miserable habit

which has ever clung to Americans of estimating a foreign, imported product of more value than the native and competing one. In reference to the introduction and use of American marble, this unpatriotic and wretched habit has exerted a most injurious influence. When Vermont marble was first offered in competition with the foreign, there were few who were willing even to test its value or to admit that it had any, especially as answering the requirements of the higher grades of use and excellence.

Its purity of color could not be questioned, for when compared with imported stones the gazer's eye could but see its high quality. Nor could one deny that its grain was fine or that it was susceptible of the most beautiful polish. Thus from one position after another were its opponents driven until it was finally conceded that comparative ability to stand exposure to the elements must decide its relative rank. That settled it, for the Italian marbles cannot resist the disintegrating forces of our climate like the native ones that are quarried on the shores of Lake Champlain.

Rutland has long been the centre of this vast

industry, so vast that no one can conceive of it
unless he visits the quarries and sees for himself. The pioneer firm is that of Sheldon &
Company, of West Rutland. It began operations in the spring of 1850, and from a small
plant has grown into mammoth proportions.
Its capacity was such as far back as 1875–76
that it was able to deliver to the national government for use in the national cemeteries *two
hundred and forty thousand headstones!* This
one contract involved the shipment of *six thousand tons* of sawn marble each year. And this
they were able to do *without interfering with
their regular business.*

To many of those who shall visit Lake Champlain, an excursion of a day to the vast marble
quarries of West Rutland, Sutherland Falls,
and Swanton, would be the most instructive
and entertaining they might take. It would
interest them to see whence are to come the
monuments, the statues, and the palaces of the
future, as grief, art, and wealth shall call them
forth. The manufacture of marble, by which
is meant the preparation of the original block
for its destined purpose, is a most interesting

study. To see with one's own eyes how the "angel hidden in the stone" is summoned forth and made to stand before the gazer in all its celestial beauty is an object lesson of the rarest sort. If you have a day to spare, ladies and gentlemen, visit the marble quarries of these noted localities.

AUTHOR'S NOTE.

ALTHOUGH it is not generally known, nevertheless it is held by those who have knowledge of the matter, that no body of water in the country affords better sport for anglers than Lake Champlain. That the subject might be intelligently and attractively treated, we enlisted the co-operation of Mr. A. Nelson Cheney of Glens Falls, N.Y., whose volume on "Fishing with the Fly," and many contributions to the press, have given him a deserved reputation in angling matters both at home and abroad, and caused him to be honored as an authority on all subjects connected with the fish and fishing of America. His essay, at our request, is written from the standpoint of personal knowledge and experience, and will be read with delight by all who are lovers of rod and reel. May it not be hoped that some day, not remote, he will favor the country with a volume on fish and fishing on Lake Champlain? It is an ample theme for a pen like his, and we know no other writer in the country who could do the work as he could do it.

THE GAME FISH AND FISHING OF LAKE CHAMPLAIN.

By A. NELSON CHENEY.

THE history, the romance, and the legends of Lake Champlain have met with greater or less recognition at the hands of those who have striven to make the fair fame of the lake known to the world, but to the angler familiar with its waters it is often surprising that its fish and its fishing have been passed over with scant courtesy. Particularly is this the case when it is considered that the lake which bears the name of Samuel Champlain affords some of the very best angling with rod and line that is to be found in all this broad land, remarkable as it is for prolificness of species and prodigality in numbers of what are known to the sportsmen as game fish. True it is, lamentably true, that the kingly salmon no longer finds its way from the sea through the St. Lawrence and

Richelieu rivers to the streams flowing into the
lake on either side; the brook-trout, *fontinalis*,
— the prince of the fountains, — if it ever was
known in the lake, has taken its departure with
the French name, *Iracosia*, applied to the water;
the lake-trout, that the Indians called *Namaycush*, has also disappeared as effectively as the
Iroquois name of the lake, *Caniaderi Guarunte*
— "the lake that is the gate of the country";
but with the departure of the *salmonidæ* — fish
of royal lineage — the gate was left ajar that
strangers might enter the water of promise, and
there remained behind and took deep root other
fish less aristocratic, but sweet of flesh, game
on the hook, fruitful of increase, strong to resist murder, outrage, and untimely death by
net, spear, and torch and other engines of
destruction that have made the salmon family
but a memory. To-day these hardy, fighting,
gamy fish abound in the lake, thrive and multiply, giving pleasure and health to thousands
who seek their capture; and who shall say it is
not the survival of the fittest?

Approaching the lake from the south, its
appearance is not inviting. The marshy shores

and the water, thick and discolored as it is by washing against banks of clay that hold it in check, are not pleasing to one who has angled in limpid waters framed in pebbly shores and backed by the green of forests; so many an angler has condemned the lake and turned back at the sight of its "tail."

It is strange, but a fact, that people living within fifty miles of Lake Champlain speak of its waters as muddy. They do not know it; and it shall be our pleasure to introduce them, and we hope others, to some of the beauties and attractions of this grand sheet of water — a Mecca for anglers.

The fish that now holds first place in the waters of the lake, and in the esteem of the angler as a rod fish, is the small-mouth black bass, *Micropterus dolomieu*. The large-mouth black bass, or Oswego bass, *Micropterus salmoides*, is also found here, but it inhabits reedy, marshy bays and creeks, and is not sought by the angler, so that hereafter by black bass we shall mean the small-mouth. This fish loves the rocks, gravel, sand, and clear water, and in the lake it finds such an abundance of suitable food that, fishing for black bass from Maine to Michigan and from Canada to Virginia, we have not found its superior, and scarcely its equal, for the table; and its game qualities are not exceeded by the black bass of any other waters. A bass hooked while the writer was fishing off Wood's Island, near St. Albans Bay, jumped clear of the water seven times before it was brought to the landing-net. There are hundreds of acres of shoals in the lake, affording the very best possible breeding-grounds for the bass, and, with anything like moderation in fishing and a due regard for the close season, its black-bass fishing should always be of the best. The black bass is the game fish of the people, because its haunts are accessible in waters of civilization, waters ploughed by crafts of commerce as well as of pleasure, and it is found at its best in broad lakes and mighty rivers, where the trout of mountain streams and secluded forest lakes would sicken and die, harried by revolving propellers and turning paddle-wheels. Being a spring-spawning fish, the eggs of the black bass hatch quickly, and as the spawning-beds and fry, when hatched, are guarded by the parent fish, the young black bass are not subjected to casualties that threaten the extermination of other species of game fish. Taking fly or bait boldly; fighting desperately when hooked; leaping from the water like the salmon and the tarpon; toothsome when prepared for the table, Nature evidently intended the black bass to be, as it is now generally accepted, the universal game fish of the United States east of the Rocky Mountains.

At the lower or northern end of the lake, east of the islands North and South Hero, or Grand Isle, as the southernmost of the Hero Islands is called; south of McQuam Bay and north of the sandbar bridge, is a portion of the lake, about twenty-one miles long north and south and five miles wide, which is very like a lake of itself, as it has but two comparatively narrow openings, the Gut and Alburgh Passage, into the main lake, to which anglers have given the title Great Back Bay.

This great bay is referred to with much justice as the home of the black bass. Within its confines are a dozen islands, and bars, shoals, or reefs which cannot be numbered. On the

north is Missisquoi Bay, which is evidently
the winter resort for many of the fishes of the
lake, because there they find water of a higher
temperature than in the lake itself.   This bay
is not only a winter resort and feeding-ground
for game fishes, but it is a breeding-ground for
fish food.   The water of Back Bay is as clear
almost as the water of famed Lake George, and
has a depth of over one hundred and fifty feet,
according to the government charts, although
the average depth is perhaps about fifty feet,
while there are acres of shoals and bars with
water from five to twenty feet deep over them.

Mt. Mansfield and Camel's Hump look down
on the bay from the Vermont side, and Mt.
Marcy, White Face, and other Adirondack
mountains look down from the New York side,
so that altogether there is a vastness about the
scene which is impressive.   The islands and
the shores of the Back Bay furnish fine camping
sites, and there are hotel accommodations for
those who object to an outing under canvas.
The fish laws of Vermont, which obtain on the
waters of Back Bay, make the legal season for
black-bass fishing from June 1 to February 1;

but no bass may be captured and retained less than ten inches in length.

June is the season for fly-fishing, for at that time the bass are on the shores and in shallow water; but later in the season if one casts a fly at nightfall or early in the morning on the shallow water over sandbars and shoals, where the bass come to feed, reasonable success may result. For bait-fishing with minnows, grasshoppers, crickets, frogs or crawfish, a rocky or pebbly shoal is selected, where the water is from ten to twenty feet deep, and there the boat is anchored. The bass of Lake Champlain are caught in remarkably shallow water, and only in the month of August is it necessary to resort to the greater depth of water mentioned. At all times bass may be caught in very shallow water by fishing on the bars and shoals before daylight in the morning and after dark at night. This is not as pleasant for the angler as good daylight, but it secures large fish. A leaf from my fishing journal will give a case in point. When first I fished the waters of Back Bay, I found it customary with the anglers assembled at a favorite resort on the shore to eat

a leisurely breakfast and get on the water about
half-past seven or eight o'clock. The bay is a
place of magnificent distances, as it requires a
pull of three or four miles for the boatman to
reach the fishing points most in favor, so that an
hour and a half more was required before the
bait was offered to the fish. This was contrary
to all teachings which point to success in
angling, or in other things, and, although the
landlord informed me that I was violating
tradition, and the boatman told me a bass never
had been taken in the lake at such a heathenish
hour, I ordered my boat to be ready an hour
before daybreak on a certain morning. I do
not think I realized before how much "sand"
it required to fly in the face of tradition, upset
custom, and do in Rome what the Romans
said, with a satisfied smile of superiority, would
bring me rich, dewy, rosy experience, but no
fish. When I came in that morning, only a
little late for the regular breakfast, there must
have been something in the appearance of the
string of black bass that my boatman placed
with some pride on the grass before the hotel
door, either the number of them or their size,

that caused the Romans to think that while the very early morning air was certainly not good to prolong the life of a big black bass, it might be of benefit to the angler. This is merely conjecture; but a few mornings later, when my boatman, Warren Greene, called me at three o'clock A. M., he whispered through the half-open door: "Joe Armstrong got up when I did, and it looks as though his man was going a-fishing."

Before I finished dressing and made a cup of coffee over a spirit-lamp, Warren was again at my door to say, "Two boats have started already, and two other guides are up and getting their boats ready." East of Wood's Island is a vast sand shoal, cone-shaped, with the island for its base, and the apex in the direction of the rising sun. At the point of the "bar," as the shoal is called, the water drops suddenly to about fifteen feet in depth, as it likewise does on the north side, but on the bar itself the water is scarcely more than six feet deep. Just at the point of the bar the fishing is considered best, particularly if there is a current. This current is made by the wind blow-

ing several days from north or south and piling
up the water in the opposite end of the bay,
when it sets back to its normal condition,
producing a decided flow like a river. The
bass are on the watch for any food that may
drift along past the point, and to strike them
at such a time means a big bag of fine fish.
The point of the bar was supposed to be fully
ripe for fishing the morning that Warren was
impatient because I waited for my cup of coffee.
The time was the 10th of August, and when we
put out from the boat-house it was in the darkness which precedes the dawn; and Warren
observed that we would reach the bar long
before we could see the shore landmarks by
which to locate the point; but he thought he
could "hit it pretty close in the dark." As we
neared the bar two boats could be seen dimly,
anchored about where we judged the point
should be; but Warren whispered that he did
not think either boat was over just the right
spot, and I hastily baited my hook with a grass-
hopper, as Warren peered here and there ahead
of the boat, hoping to see something to guide
him to the location we were seeking. I cast my

'hopper on the water, dragging it behind the boat, when suddenly it was snapped up by a hungry bass. And I turned to Warren and told him to drop anchor quickly and let the boat swing back with the current about fifteen feet. There was a splash as the anchor went down at the bow, and another as the bass jumped at the stern, and the boat dropped back the length of the slack-rope as Warren stepped toward me with the landing-net. The bass was now in, now out of the water, but neither of us could see the fish when it was out any more than when it was in, and I finally reeled it to the boat, and the net was placed under it by an exercise of faith — a three and one-half pound fish, just the fighting size. The current was strong and the bass greedy, for another 'hopper on the hook was taken as quickly as the first, and the bass as quickly lost from not being well hooked. There was no sound of revelry from either of the other boats as I hooked the third bass, which came to the net after a struggle, and I thought we might wait for more light, which shortly came stealing up over the Green Mountains, faintly, but sufficient to show the

bass when hooked and led to the net. Before
the sun fairly appeared above the hills, I noticed
the light color of the bass, which was evidence
that the fish had been on the white sand all
night (a bass will quickly take on the general
color of the bottom on which it rests), and that
we were fishing directly over the bar. This I
remarked to Warren, and he glanced around,
chuckled quietly, shut one eye knowingly,
jerked his head over his left shoulder, and
said, —

"Do you see the big pine square over the
north gable of the barn on the island and the
notch in the hill in line with the point on
Potter Island?" Sure enough! The boat was
anchored as fairly over the point of the bar as
Warren could have anchored it at high noon
with the sun shining and all the landmarks
located with a theodolite. The other boats
were taking an occasional bass, but they had
missed the point and they knew it only too
well. A bass that proved to weigh four and a
quarter pounds when it was landed, took my
bait, and, as he jumped from the water and
showed his dark green sides in the sunlight, I

said, " Here is a bass that has just come on to
the bar from the grass for its breakfast, and
now we shall have to wait for such as come
straggling along to feed ; we have cleaned the
bar of such bass as have been here all night."
This proved true, and after waiting for a time
we moved about one hundred yards to a patch
of grass bottom with an occasional water-weed
growing near to the surface. Casting the
baited hook over, there was no response on the
part of fish of any kind, for this is famous yel-
low-perch ground, and I concluded there was a
big bass " there or thereabouts " which held the
perch in reserve and made them backward
about coming forward. The diagnosis was
correct, for there was a bite, and the next
moment a " barn-door " (any one who fishes in
Lake Champlain will soon learn that a " barn-
door " is a black bass of the largest calibre)
was shaking its head in the air with the hook
fast in its jaw. As Warren put the net under
the fish and brought it into the boat, he said it
was a " barn-door," sure enough ; and as he
hooked the scales through its mouth and they
marked full five pounds, he added, " That's 'old

glory,' the biggest bass taken in the bay this year." When we went in, we had twenty-six black bass, which weighed fifty-six pounds ten ounces, and eighteen of them weighed just ten pounds less, or forty-six pounds ten ounces.

North of Diadama Island is another shoal, of pebbles instead of sand, and here there is excellent bass-fishing, particularly at night or morning. West of Diadama is a clump of big rocks, and west of Diadama shoal is another, where as good fishing may be found as any one could wish. Gull Rock and Long Reef, and the middle reef between Gull Rock and the north end of Butler's Island, and in the cove at the south of Butler's Island, is good fishing. Pop Squash furnishes fine fishing also, but one should have a boatman to show him a score of good places where large bass and plenty of them may be taken.

The yellow perch from this pure, clear water make an excellent pan fish; they are really sweeter than the bass (if I may be forgiven the heresy), and they can be taken in large numbers wherever there is grass bottom or weeds. It is the custom to despise the yellow perch where the black-bass fishing is so good 'as at Back Bay, but, feeling hungry for perch one day, I went with Warren to the grass where the five-pound bass was taken, and caught seventy-six large perch, and. as the Indian said of his venison killed out of season, " call it bulldog or mountain sheep, it is good to eat."

A fish that is esteemed by some more highly for the table than the black bass is the pike-perch, or wall-eyed pike. *Stizostedium vitreum.* The pike-perch has a cousin, *S. Canadense,* popularly known as Sauger, or Sandpike, more beautiful in coloring than the pike-perch, but smaller, as it rarely grows to exceed fifteen inches. while the pike-perch grows to ten pounds and upward. Both of these fish are found in Lake Champlain. and the legal season for catching them is the same as that of the black bass. Pike-perch are frequently taken while fishing for black bass, but to make a business of catching them the best time is June and late in the fall. They are caught by still-fishing with live minnows. Even in June and late autumn, the fishing for pike-perch is not as good as it is through the ice in winter, for they

go on the sandbars in great numbers three
months before the spawning season, which is in
March and April, and there remain until they
spawn and disperse. They are very prolific,
casting two or three hundred thousand eggs,
and they spawn when they reach a pound in
weight. Like all spring-spawning fish, except
the black bass, their eggs furnish food for other
predaceous fishes. The black bass is an exception because, as already stated, they guard
their spawning-beds; the bullhead and sunfish
being the only other fish that exercise this care
over eggs and young. A fish that can scarcely
be called a game fish, yet is taken occasionally
on the hook in Lake Champlain, strange as the
statement may appear, is the lake shad, so-
called, but which really is the whitefish of the
great lakes, *Coregonus clupeiformis*. This fish
is protected by the laws of Vermont from
November 1 to November 15, and the law is
about as effective as that which protects the
black bass, for the whitefish spawns as late as
the first week in December, the greater number
spawning from the 15th of November to the
1st of December, and the black bass spawns

during nearly the entire month of June. The laws mean well, but do not actually cover what they are intended to cover, viz., the breeding-season. It is not so unusual for whitefish to take a baited hook as it might be supposed. They are caught in winter through the ice in one or more of the Adirondack lakes, in such numbers as to make it worth the while fishing for them, and one angler has taken a number in Back Bay in summer, and he told me that with their delicate mouths they were not an insignificant fish on the rod ; and certainly there is no more delicately delicious fish on the table than a whitefish fresh from the water. The mascalonge, *Esox nobilior*, the nobler pike, is sometimes taken in Lake Champlain, and if the New York Fish Commission is successful in cultivating the fish artificially at Chautauqua Lake, it is to be hoped that the same work may be taken up at Lake Champlain, and the water made to teem with this great game fish. There are parts of the lake admirably suited to this fish, and it is well worth the experiment to make it common in the water.

The pike, *Esox lucius*, commonly called

pickerel, also called fresh-water shark, slimy snake, and other choice names, is omnipresent in Lake Champlain. It bobs up when least expected, and a hook baited with a live minnow is never safe from its long jaws. A gentleman casting a fly on Diadama bar for black bass announced to a friend who was with him, that there was a supreme satisfaction in fly-fishing for bass, for even if the bass did not rise to the fly the pickerel would not, and if there was any particular fish that he cordially disliked it was a pickerel. The first fish that he hooked was a pickerel that tore his fly in tatters. While the pickerel is generally regarded with disfavor by those who seek the black bass, it must be confessed that a pickerel from clear. cold water in the autumn. if properly dressed. by some other fellow, makes good eating ; but these conditions do not exist usually as do those other conditions of warm, thick water, and the odor of water weeds and rank vegetation and general sliminess that hangs about the fish. A fish that in any other .country than America would be considered a sporting fish is the chub or fall fish, *Semotilus bullaris*. It is a beautiful

silvery fish, fights well on the hook, takes fly
and bait, and it is found in schools in Lake
Champlain, but to the bass-fisher it is a nui-
sance. When hooked, the fall fish acts not
unlike the brook trout, and Professor Goode
says that in Massachusetts it is called the
"cousin trout," because of its trout-like habits.
Yet this fish is caught only to be thrown away.

Another fish found in the lake must have a
short notice, although it is anything but a game
fish. This fish is called the sheeps-head, but it
is the fresh-water drum, *Haploidonotus grun-
niens*, and is as worthless for any purpose as
any fish that I know. If it is distinguished for
anything it is for its ear-bones, which are called
"lucky-bones." These bones, two in each fish,
are about the size of a nickel and of the texture
of ivory, but pearly white; and have plainly
marked on the surface a letter L, which certainly stands for lucky-bone. They may possi-
bly be lucky, but they do not work in pairs.

I had been fishing in Back Bay for a week
with two Texas friends, and during the last
day's fishing a "sheeps-head" was taken in one
of the boats, and the boatman took out the

lucky-bones from the head of the fish and presented one to one of the Texans and the other to the writer, " for luck." We gibed the third member of our party, the major, because he had no visible, tangible, material evidence of luck in his whole outfit, but promised he should share in our dividends — and he did. He declared that he did not desire to have any " mullet-head luck," and that the letter L in our cases stood for lunatics. The next morning, we started from St. Albans to go through Lakes Champlain and George, and at Burlington reached the steamboat dock in time to get a square view of the stern of the Vermont steaming away to Ticonderoga, and the major growled something about " luck," which did not begin with g. We were told that by crossing the lake to Westport on another steamer, we could catch the Montreal train, which would overtake the boat, and we joyfully told the major that the lucky-bones would work all right when we had mastered the combination.

Our steamer reached the Westport dock seventeen minutes after the train had steamed away southward; and there the major offered to buy the lucky-bones, and the negotiations might have ended in a riot if the major had not happened to see a man on the dock with a fine string of black bass, which he went to ask about, and found they were caught from the dock.

We ordered a carriage to take us to An Sable Chasm, and while waiting for it, the owner of one lucky-bone bantered the owner of the other to run a foot-race, with the major for finish judge, for a cool, well-favored, robust, carefully selected bottle of the juice of the grape, extra dry. The race was run, and the major decided it a dead heat. Three times he ordered it run over, because it was a dead heat, although there were several yards between the runners at the finish, before we discovered that he was trying to kill the contestants. When we reached the hotel we found we had time to go through the chasm before dinner, and started at once. At the Grand Flume we found a boat but no boatman, and the major insisted that "this *is* luck; but *such* luck!" We reached the outlet without "going up the flume," but there was no wagon to take us to the hotel.

The major glared, but speech failed him, and when finally we did get to the hotel, late for a hot dinner but just in time for a cold one, the storm-cloud burst with a clatter that would have made the dogs of war stick their tails between their hinder legs, and strike out for the brush. The riot act read something after this style: "This is Saturday, and our only chance to get to our families is the midnight express from Montreal, provided we can drive to the depot without the horses running away, which I doubt. On the train are men, women, and children that never harmed either one of you, never heard of you and never wish to, and they will be sleeping peacefully, innocently, never dreaming that each of you has a lucky-bone in his pocket, and it is a bad night for the train to jump the track. You start to-night, and I shall wait until Monday, for I cannot trust myself on a railway train with those lucky-bones. You have tried them on water and on land, and they do not work; neither of you can fly, to try them in the air; sell them to me, and I will send them to a man who stole a pail of bait-fish from me at Lake George, and they will ruin his fishing forever." We knew the man, and sold out our luck. This experience is given as a warning, and it may be added that directly after the bait-appropriator received the lucky-bones he lost the biggest fish that ever he hooked.

Something like fifteen years ago I was in Port Henry in March or April, and the hotel-keeper where I dined regretted that he was unable to give me some "ice-fish" for my dinner. It was to me a new fish, and I was then informed that they were comparatively new to Lake Champlain, but were caught through the ice in great quantities at that season. A description of the fish made me think that they were the smelt. *Osmerus mordax,* and when, later, samples were sent to me, that is what they proved to be. They were then caught near Port Henry and at Westport. I have since learned of their being taken opposite Burlington and at Plattsburg. At one point they were called frost-fish, but where that was I do not recall. If they are taken in one part of the lake they should be found in other parts, and I presume they are. They furnish fishing at a season when nothing better offers, and every one knows that they are good when fried in fat like a cruller and served with sauce tartare. During the coming spring the United States Fish Commission will furnish a million lake-trout fry to be planted in Lake Champlain, and there seems no good reason why this fine fish should not thrive therein and furnish excellent angling and a new and choice food fish. Trolling for lake trout is not fly-fishing, but when a fifteen-pound *Namaycush* is hooked at the surface on a light rod it is fishing "good enough for the Jones family." A sentiment which upholds the fish laws as just and proper is rapidly growing with all people. Canadian authorities are working in harmony with the Vermont Fish Commission to stop the netting of fish in Missisquoi Bay, that vast breeding and feeding ground, and the prospect for good and varied fishing in Lake Champlain was never better since the salmon disappeared than to-day.

Recalling the pleasures we have enjoyed, most heartily do we commend the splendid rod-fishing to be found in Lake Champlain to brother anglers. To the fly-fisher we make no sugges-

tion as to lures, for his fly-book will contain,
somewhere between its covers, just the combination of feathers, silk, mohair, and tinsel, when
deftly cast, to draw to the landing-net black
bass to satisfy the most exacting. To the bait-
fisher we will say that on the shores of the lake
and in the small streams thereof, there may be
found in abundance the shiniest minnows for
early fishing, the biggest and yellowest grasshoppers and fattest and blackest crickets for
midsummer fishing, and the greenest frogs and
thinnest-shelled crayfish for later fishing.

To those who visit fair Champlain and partake
of and enjoy her wealth of game fishes, her
health-giving air, her glorious, sunny days and
peaceful, restful nights, may there come again
and again, in the language of the lamented
Westwood, the nineteenth-century Walton,—

> "Oh, the pleasant roaming
> Homeward through the gloaming!
> Oh, the heavy creel, alack! Oh, the joyful greeting!
> Oh, the jokes and laughter,
> And the sound sleep after,
> And the happy, happy dreams, all the sport repeating!"

www.ingramcontent.com/pod-product-compliance
Lightning Source LLC
Chambersburg PA
CBHW030641030726
47497CB00006B/1892